OHIO
DOMINICAN
UNIVERSITY™

SINCE 1911

Donated by
Floyd Dickman

the
Dark Ground

the dark ground

BOOK ONE OF THE DARK GROUND TRILOGY

Gillian Cross

DUTTON CHILDREN'S BOOKS

NEW YORK

Copyright © 2004 by Gillian Cross

CIP Data is available.

Published in the United States 2004 by Dutton Children's Books,
a division of Penguin Young Readers Group
345 Hudson Street, New York, New York 10014
www.penguin.com

Originally published in Great Britain 2004 by Oxford University Press, London.
Printed in USA · Designed by Tim Hall
ISBN: 0-525-47350-5
First American Edition
1 3 5 7 9 10 8 6 4 2

the
Dark Ground

Before

1

A RAVINE CUT INTO THE GROUND, RUNNING FROM NORTH TO south. It was too wide to jump across and too long to travel around. Its overgrown banks went down sheer into the darkness.

On its western side, a bare, ridged tree rose out of the ground, growing clear of the black forest beyond. It stood tall and pale in the moonlight, topped by a crown of dead branches.

From high up in the crown, someone whistled.

Cam stepped out of the shadows on the eastern side, with the others close behind her. They all stared up at the dead tree across the ravine, hunting for Zak's silhouette among the branches. He called out to them, and the words drifted down like sounds from another world.

"Once it was like this. Remember?"

No! said a voice in Cam's head. *No, I won't, I won't—*

But it was too late. Zak had spoken the word they never used, and her brain filled with forbidden images. She saw herself racing over the grass, with the world turning under her and the sky wide open above her head. Her hands moved powerfully, commanding fire and water. She soared among the clouds.

Be quiet, Zak. Be QUIET!

But he was way up in the branches, too high to reach. He was beyond her orders.

"Remember," he called down. "You were up in the air—above the tops of the trees. Remember the dazzle of the sun and the space and the speed. You were *there*. Remember . . ."

She couldn't stop him. None of them could stop him. He was beyond the gaping ravine, at the top of the tall, dead trunk. Only Zak could climb well enough to reach those high, cupped branches.

"Remember . . ." he said again. The sound was relentless. Unbearable.

Cam put her fingers in her ears, turning away, but she could still hear him. They all heard. *Remember, remember . . .* The word battered at them until the darkness vibrated with anger and pain, and there was no way of stopping it. No way of silencing Zak.

Except the rope.

The rope ends were on the ground, at Cam's feet. The great, twelve-strand rope stretched across the ravine and back again, looping twice around the trunk of Zak's tree. As he called again, Cam stooped blindly, grabbing at one of the ends.

The others stooped, too, jostling to find places. A dozen hands clamped around each length of rope.

"Remember," Zak shouted—and Cam began to pull, straining at the rope. Putting all her rage and pain into that single action.

Zak's voice grew louder. "Re*mem*ber! You were high in the air! Above the tops of the trees, in the full dazzle of the sun! But—all in a flash—you came tumbling down, out of the music and the buzz and the energy, into deep silence. Out of the light and into the cold shadows. Re*mem*ber! Re*mem*ber!"

They were all pulling now. Their movements followed the rhythm of his voice, and the trunk started to sway and creak, gathering momentum as they heaved. Up in the sky, among the top branches, Zak threw his weight forward, toward the ravine.

"Re*mem*ber!"

The trunk gave way, keeling over suddenly, and Zak scrambled through the branches, screaming one word with all the air in his lungs, "DOWN!"

He rode out the fall, straddling the trunk, but the others were caught in the whip of branches. As the tree swept down toward them, Cam was knocked clean off her feet. She clenched her fists, fighting the sound that welled up inside her.

No! she thought fiercely. *Zak, why did you have to—oh damn, I'm not going to—*but it was impossible to stay quiet. As the tree fell, the others began to wail with rage and pain. Cam struggled for a moment and then opened her mouth and howled, giving in to the darkness.

Zak fell past her, in the branches, so close that she saw the blue flash of his eyes. The great tree came down across the gulf, spanning it like a bridge, and crashed, headfirst, onto the dark ground.

2

HIGH IN THE CLOUDS, SOMETHING SLAMMED INTO ROBERT'S sleeping brain and he woke suddenly, in a rush of adrenaline. His mind was churning with images of falling, of tumbling out of the sky in a roar of broken, burning metal. He smelled the scorching and felt the rush of air against his helpless skin as he fell. . . .

"*Stop* it!" Emma hissed fiercely into his ear. She grabbed at his arm and shook it, digging in with her fingers. "Be *quiet!*"

He hadn't known he was making noise. He tried to move his head and found that it had slid sideways, wedged between the seat and the window shade. The engine noise vibrated in his ears, and his neck was stiff and aching.

Falling . . .

He sat up and rubbed at his cheek. "What happened?"

"Nothing happened," Emma said crossly. "You were just dreaming. Making a terrible, moaning noise."

"I was—"

Robert couldn't get the words out. The falling and the noise and the burning were still real and savage in his mind, and he needed to talk about them. But not to Emma. His sister was the last person in the world he would choose to tell. She wouldn't understand, and she would just say the same things, all over again. *It was only a dream. Nothing happened.*

He flexed his shoulders and looked around. She was right, of course. In a way. They were sitting side by side in the dark-

8

ened cabin, with the engines flying the plane steadily through the night. He could hear Mom and Dad talking quietly in the seats behind. He could see a flight attendant moving calmly down the cabin. Nothing had happened.

And yet he had been falling in fire and darkness. Every cell of his body was jarred, and his heart was thumping. Was that nothing?

Turning away from Emma, he slid up the shade to look out of the window. The rising sun flared into his eyes so that he ducked his head, squinting to escape the dazzle. They were flying over a mass of trees that stretched in all directions. A river snaked out from the horizon, glinting golden where it caught the light, but the ground under the trees was dark and hidden.

Emma leaned across his body, pushing him out of the way so that she could see.

"Wow!" she said. "Isn't that lovely? It's just like a photo."

"No, it's not!" Robert pushed her away angrily. "Don't be stupid!"

The rush of fury took him by surprise, but it was her fault for talking nonsense. *It's just like a photo.* What did she mean? A photograph was just an image—flat colors on a piece of shiny paper. There was nothing behind the surface.

What they could see through the window was completely different. It was *real*.

If they swooped down twenty-five thousand feet, the tangled mass of treetops would separate into a pattern of interwoven branches, of twigs and leaves and intricate, ridged bark. If they dived through that, into the shadows, there would be a whole, secret world of animals and plants, and of streams and earth. And, deeper still, there were insects and fungi and tiny micro-organisms, getting smaller and smaller, in unimaginable complexity.

He and Emma were the ones who were unreal. They were floating high above the trees in a pressurized capsule, surrounded by strangers. The air they breathed was recycled, and the temperature around them was artificially controlled. Every surface he could see was molded into smooth, unnatural curves, and beyond those curves was—nothing. Except the cold and empty sky.

The plane felt safe and ordinary, but it would take only a crack to shatter that safety and plunge them headlong through the air. *Falling and burning . . .*

He pressed his forehead against the window, struggling to look down through the trees into the hidden, real ground underneath them. But he couldn't do it.

"What's gotten into you?" Emma said.

It was dark, and there was noise and fire. . . . The words burned in Robert's head, but he couldn't speak them. The dark and the fire and the falling were *real,* like the trees and the river. But he couldn't explain that to Emma. She would give him a scornful, superior stare and go on talking about dreams and photos and what time the plane was going to land.

And she would think he was pathetic.

As usual.

Reaching forward, he snatched the travel kit out of the pocket in front of him.

"I'm going to brush my teeth," he said abruptly. He stood up and squeezed his way out into the aisle, pushing past Emma and the person in the next seat, without giving them a chance to move.

He thought he had his expression under control, but there must have been something odd about it. When he reached the bathroom, the man who was coming out gave him a long, strange look. His eyes were blue and very clear. Robert turned away from them, hiding his face as he went through the open door.

The restroom was in the center of the plane—a neat, cramped cubicle with no window and everything made to fit into the smallest possible space. Laying his travel kit on the shelf, Robert took out the toothbrush and toothpaste. He unscrewed the top of the tube and squeezed a short length of toothpaste onto his brush.

But he could still feel eyes watching him . . .

He looked up quickly and found himself staring straight into the face in the mirror. *What's the matter with me? I can't be scared of myself.* But there was something unsettling about the reflection. Putting his toothbrush down, he leaned closer, peering at it.

His own eyes peered back at him. They were gray green, striped in a dozen places with faint, brown lines. The pattern was infinitely familiar—but today there was something different about it.

A face was looking back at him down the black tunnel of the pupils.

It was a tiny, strange face, almost too small to see. He moved his head and it kept time, moving with him, its own eyes as sharp as pinpoints. When he lifted his hand toward it, a minute, pale hand came up in answer, stretching out to him.

Who is it? he thought. He could see the mirrored hand trembling in the glass. *Is that my face? My hand?*

His own hand was trembling, too. Half of him wanted to look away, but he couldn't make his eyes disconnect. Taking a slow, deliberate breath, he reached out farther, nearer the glass. And nearer still . . . until his real hand met the mirror hand, fingertip to fingertip—

—and a shock went through him, jolting his whole body.

The strange face exploded forward, swooping out of the darkness. For a split second, in a flash of clear, dazzling blue, he saw his own face reflected in its eyes.

Then the darkness flared into his face, blotting out everything. It exploded around him, grating against his eyes and grinding into his head. Air and vibration beat at him, until he was shaken from the inside outward.

Noise roared into every cell, jarring his bones and burning up his blood, and raw heat blasted against the surface of his skin.

Then a long, wrenching twist wound up the spirals of his body, squeezing in and down and in and down and inanddownandinananddownand—

And a deeper darkness came up to meet him.

I

Alone

3

HE CAME TO SUDDENLY, SHOCKED AND SHIVERING. ONE moment he was unconscious and the next he was sitting up in a litter of wet, rotting vegetation, with the wind scouring his bare skin.

He was cold and naked, and his whole, aching body was covered with scratches. The damp air around him smelled of decay. The ground ran away into shadows. Looking up, he saw a tangle of branches arching far above his head, closing out the light.

He had absolutely no idea where he was.

He remembered walking down the plane toward the restroom. But after that—nothing. It was like looking into a thick fog full of hazy shapes that slid away when he tried to focus. There had been a blur of pain and a dazzle of light—

And then an exploding, overwhelming darkness.

He began to test out his body, checking the bones. Working each joint to be sure that it was still functioning.

Fingers? Eight (plus two thumbs), all whole and agile.

Toes? They wiggled reassuringly.

Arms? Legs? Nothing wrong there.

Back? He winced as he moved and felt the long, raw patch running down the left-hand side. Was it a burn or a scrape? He tried looking over his shoulder, but he couldn't see, and he had no way of finding out.

He was shivering harder now, not from shock, but from

sheer cold. Within a few moments that had driven everything else out of his mind. He had to get warm. It was more urgent than hunger, more important than understanding. He had to cover himself up.

But how?

He was lying half submerged in a chilly, disintegrating mass of leaf fragments, as thick and heavy as wet leather. The tangled branches over his head were dark and dripping, and a break in the canopy showed a glimpse of threatening sky.

He had to find some kind of shelter.

Squelching in old leaf-sludge, he dragged himself onto his feet and looked around. He was in the middle of a strange, gloomy forest. Its floor was wet and barren, covered with leaf litter.

Out of the leaf litter, jagged, gnarled tree trunks thrust vigorously upward. They grew in clumps, three or four together, splaying apart and rising high above his head, with branches that curved like great, stone ribs. They wove in and out of each other, and their coarse, tarnished leaves shut out the sun. It was impossible to see anything beyond them.

The wet ground had no clues to give him either. There was no sign of a trail. Nothing to show how he had come into the forest and no path to lead him out. Everything looked the same, whichever way he turned.

He began to struggle forward over the leaves, choosing a direction at random. It was slow and tiring. The brown mess sagged and squelched under him, and twice he slipped and landed on his hands and knees. His limbs ached and his back hurt. Every step was an effort.

He was just beginning to feel that the forest was endless,

that he might as well give up, when he caught a glimpse of something different, off to his left. A patch of light, broken by pale, vertical lines. He slithered toward it and found himself at a break in the canopy.

Behind him the dark forest was full of vigorous, arching trees and the strong smell of decay. Ahead the ground was quite different. Dozens of pale trees rose up into the sky, almost impossibly tall, hardly branching until the very top. Their trunks were straight and slender, and they had a dry, brittle look. Their stunted, spindly branches had begun to disintegrate, splitting open to spill out long white fibers.

Every one of the trees was dead.

They rose out of a wilderness of tall, bent plants that looked like old bamboo. The rain had beaten down their jointed stems and plastered the leaf strips one over another, molding the plants into high, soggy mounds. He thought he might somehow use the leaves to cover himself, but when he pulled at one it was coarse and tough, and it scratched his hands.

It was quite dead. Everything was dead.

He was standing on the edge of a ghost wood.

The only living thing was a long, tough creeper, thicker than his arm. Its spiraling stems had reached out greedily, looping from one tree to another and scrambling upward.

On the far side of the pale wood, it had pulled some of the dry trees sideways, roping them around so that half a dozen leaned together. Farther on, the creeper's weight had brought down a couple of other trees. It grew over them in a thick mat, with their odd, split branches sticking through.

The strands that spilled out of them had a soft, silky look, and Robert's heart jumped suddenly. He could see that they might be within his reach and he began to struggle toward them, fighting his way between the clumps of bamboo.

The ground was covered with a network of tough bamboo stems, and it was hard going, but he had a purpose now. He hardly noticed how the rough bamboo leaves scraped at his skin. He was more concerned by a sudden darkening that seemed to threaten rain. He wanted to reach that silky floss before it was drenched and useless. Rubbing impatiently at his scratched legs, he battled on over the roots and the creeping stalks.

When he reached the fallen trees, he found that their branches were higher than he had thought. But by standing on tiptoe, he could just touch the lowest one. Straining upward, he buried his hands in the soft, thick floss and tugged. A great clump of it came loose, tangled with seeds. He pulled it down and twisted the long strands together, feeling their warmth.

He had had grand ideas of making them into thread, maybe even weaving some kind of cloth. But as soon as he had them in his hands, he realized that all that was a hopeless fantasy. He would have to settle for something much more primitive.

He reached up and pulled down more of the floss. Without bothering to pick out the seeds, he rubbed the silky strands together, turning the whole mass in on itself until it hung together in a huge, matted bundle. It was bulky, but very light and soft.

Parting it with his hands, he burrowed in, pulling it on over his head, like a shirt, and pushing his arms out through the sides. Then he worked away at it, tucking and knotting to close up the gaps. The result was awkward and comic—more like a sheep's fleece than a garment—but it covered him from the neck to the knees, and he was immediately warmer.

Making the fleece had given him something to focus on. As soon as it was done, his energy drained away. He was exhausted. It seemed sensible to gather more floss, before the rain started, but he couldn't make himself reach up to pull it down.

He couldn't face the effort of struggling back under the dark trees either, but the temperature was dropping fast and he needed some kind of shelter. Going down on all fours, he pushed his way into the nearest bamboo clump, wriggling between the tough stems and the jagged leaves that caught at his fleece and scratched his arms and face.

The stalks inside the clump were damp but not soft. They grew close together, and he squatted awkwardly between them, wedging himself into place and pulling his arms inside his fleece for warmth. The moment he stopped moving, he realized that he was hungry and desperately thirsty. But he was too tired to cope with that. He closed his eyes—*just for a second*—and fell asleep instantly, in spite of his uncomfortable position.

The last thing he heard was a dull, thudding noise as heavy raindrops began to fall on the bamboo over his head.

WHEN HE WOKE UP, IT WAS NIGHT. IN HIS SLEEP HE HAD fallen sideways, jamming his head against the tough stalks. Still half dazed, he wriggled upright and crawled out of the bamboo clump, pulling his fleece close against his body. It was damp now, but it felt comforting.

The moon was high overhead, round and full. And it was the same moon as always, with the same blurry, familiar face. Looking up at it, Robert almost cried with relief.

At least I'm in the right world.

The pale trees were white where the moon lit them. Their black shadows rippled over the ground, running up the sides of the bamboo clumps. The moonlight caught the sides of the clumps, outlining their leaves with shadows, so that each one lay in its place, clear and sharp edged.

And everywhere—on each branch and seedpod, along the edge of every blade of bamboo and every twist of creeper—great, rounded drops of water hung gleaming in the moonlight.

Robert put his cheek up to the nearest drop. It nestled against his skin like a soft, cold balloon. The shape held until he turned toward it, opening his mouth. Then it broke, and the water ran over his tongue and down his dusty throat.

In a kind of trance, he moved forward under the pale, dead trees, drinking cold light. Quenching his thirst with moon water, one drop at a time.

As he moved, the fleece scratched at his skin. Fumbling among the fibers, he pulled out a pointed seed, about the size of his thumb. It had a thick, brown husk to protect it, but the husk cracked easily between his teeth. The kernel inside was sweet and soft enough to chew. When he had eaten it, he searched through the fleece for another. And another.

It was like walking through a dream, under the distant eye of the moon. For that moment, he had everything he needed. As he ate and drank, he was aware that nothing had been solved. He was still lost and alone, without any idea of how he was going to survive. Soon he would have to confront what had happened and try to make plans.

But not yet.

4

THE NEXT WAKING WAS HARSH AND UNCOMFORTABLE. HE HAD crawled back into the bamboo clump to sleep again, and when he opened his eyes it was daylight, and he was wet through to the skin. Last night's raindrops had trickled along the leaves and down the jointed stalks, soaking into his hair and his fleece and the ground underneath him. If he stayed where he was, there was no hope of getting dry.

He crawled out of the clump, hoping to find a patch of sunlight. But it was a gray day, cold and almost still, and once he was outside he began losing heat fast. The fleece felt soggy and unpleasant, and he stripped it off and hung it up to drip on one of the creeper stems.

For the first time—now that he had slept and eaten—he felt clearheaded. He jogged on the spot to warm himself up, and, as he jogged, he tried to figure out where he was. And what had put him there.

He had been in a plane with Emma and his parents. He had gotten up to go to the restroom, and then—

And then *something* had happened. Something so cataclysmic that his mind rejected all attempts to picture it. Each time he tried, his head filled with an agonizing jumble of noise and panic and physical shock. It wasn't that he didn't remember. He remembered *so well* that his whole body relived the pain and the vibration, the roaring and the rushing chaos. But his brain refused to make sense of what he was remembering. It cut straight from the seat in the plane to the moment when he had opened his eyes under the dark trees, alone and naked and cold. With no idea where he was.

He looked left and right, up and down, gazing at the dead silk trees and the heavy, twisted creeper. He scuffed his feet against the wet, bamboo stalks and turned around to stare at the black forest behind him, with its massive, curving branches. Everything he saw was utterly strange.

And every time he breathed in, he smelled damp and rot. The wet leaves at the center of the bamboo mound, the leathery debris in the dark wood—they were all breaking down and decaying. The atmosphere was thick with the stench of death and remaking, like the air in a rainforest.

A cold rainforest?

The fleece that hooked over the creeper dripped on and on as he struggled to make sense of where he was. And how he had got there.

The plane must have crashed.

He didn't remember a crash, but that had to be the explanation. There must have been an explosion. Something so terrifying that his brain had wiped it out.

But if that was right—where were the others? Where were Mom and Dad and Emma—and all those other people, rows and rows of them, men and women and children? What had happened to them?

Maybe the plane had blown apart in midair, flinging out passengers in all directions. Perhaps, if he searched, he would find a wrecked fuselage. A radio.

Other survivors.

Maybe they weren't far away. . . .

He let the fantasy run until he could almost see the metal sides of the plane glinting through the trees. Until he fooled himself that he could hear voices in the distance, shouting his name.

Robert! Where are you? Robeeeeeerrrrt . . .

He knew he was imagining the sounds, but he put his head back and yelled, as loudly as he could.

"I'M HERE! IT'S ROBERT! IS THERE ANYONE THERE?"

His voice sounded thin and shrill. The dark forest drank up his words and the pale wood mocked him with silence. There was no answer. His shouting had not made any difference.

Except inside his head.

Until he actually heard that useless shout, disappearing into the silence, he had not really grasped that he was on his own. Somewhere at the back of his mind, he had been waiting to be found. Waiting for the police or the army or the Rainforest Rescue to come parachuting in to save him. But there was nobody. He had made as much noise as he could, and no one had answered.

He was on his own. And being cold and hungry weren't the worst things that could happen.

He could die. Quite easily.

HE STOPPED JOGGING THEN AND STOOD STARING AT THE DEAD trees in front of him. Not thinking or moving. Just taking it in. It was a long time before he could make himself think about what to do next. He needed so many things that he didn't know where to start.

Food.

Clothes.

Shelter and warmth.

A better source of water.

A way of keeping safe.

His brain mocked him with images of technology. *If I had a knife . . . if I had an ax . . . some matches . . . a tarpaulin . . .* He knew dozens of things about surviving in the wilderness, but every one of them needed something beyond a naked, human body. He had no tools, no instructions—nothing.

He was going to die.

It must have happened thousands of times before. Millions. Lots of people stuck out on their own without the right gear, all through history. People dying of hunger and thirst and cold and infection in solitary, hostile places where there was no one to hear or care. They just died, and that was it.

That was what the world was *like*.

BY THE TIME HE CAME OUT OF THAT ONE, THE SUN HAD broken through the clouds. The fleece was still damp but his skin was dry, and his mood changed all of a sudden. What was the point of spending his last few days whining? If he was going to die, he might as well do it as comfortably as possible.

That meant finding a safe place to sleep and keep dry when it rained. He needed a shelter where he could store food and try to stay warm.

A cave would have been ideal, but it didn't seem like cave country. There were plenty of trees, and he knew (in theory) how to make a lean-to—but he couldn't do anything without a knife to cut the poles. He felt like someone running around and around a maze, hitting dead ends whichever way he turned.

There had to be a way. Animals didn't have knives or nails or ropes, but they found shelter everywhere. They made nests or dug burrows. He must be able to do something like that.

He looked up at the straight, pale trees, but he couldn't see any way of climbing them. And the ground under his feet was thick with interwoven bamboo stems. He didn't like the idea of trying to dig through those, especially without a spade.

Leaving his fleece to dry, he picked his way between the bamboo clumps, heading for the place where the creeper had pulled the pale trees together. They made a rough tepee shape and, looking at it from a distance, he wondered whether he could use that as the basis for a shelter. The huge, thick bamboo leaves would be ideal for weaving in and out between the sloping trunks.

It looked like a good idea, but the moment he stepped into the circle of leaning trees, he realized that it was another fantasy. The tree trunks shot up into the air, twenty times as tall as he was. It would have taken weeks to cut enough leaves to make the walls.

Even if he'd had a knife.

He kicked at the ground, discouraged and disappointed. It would have been such a good place. Even as they were, without any weaving, the trees made a kind of screen. He felt hidden inside the circle. Protected. The trees had shaded the ground and stunted the bamboo that grew there so that it was thin and weak and easy to beat down. He would have had plenty of space to move about in.

It took him almost half an hour to realize that it was an ideal place to dig.

If he burrowed down, he could make himself a dugout, with the trees for added shelter. They had already done some of the work for him by stunting the bamboo. He could see bare earth between the crawling stems and, when he prodded at it, the ground felt soft and damp.

He knelt down and began to scrabble with his hands. He wanted to uproot some of the bamboo first to make a clear space. But the stems were too strong for him to break, and they cut his fingers. After a while he gave that up and found a place where the earth was already bare. With his hands first, and then using a stone, he scraped away, making a small, deep hole.

Underground the bamboo roots spread everywhere. They were as thick as his arm and very stringy, and they formed a tough mat, just below the surface of the ground. He scooped out the earth, trying to get below them. He thought he might be able to loosen the roots from underneath and roll the whole thing back in a single piece.

But it went much deeper than he expected. He dug on and on, down and down. By the time he was level with the lowest roots, he could hardly see over the top of the hole. And he was exhausted again.

And hungry. And thirsty.

But he didn't want to give up. He crouched down and worked his hands under the root mat, heaving at it to try and loosen it a bit. There was no movement at all. The roots spread in every direction, weaving over and under each other and anchoring themselves tightly in the ground. He would have to dig a much larger hole to have any chance of working them loose. And even if he did manage it, the root mat was much too thick and heavy to roll back in the way he had planned.

He nearly gave up then. It would have been easy to crawl back into the wet, bamboo clump and curl up, waiting to die. *I can't do it. I'm not strong enough. It was a stupid plan.*

He knew that voice in his head. *What makes you think you can do anything?* He'd heard it a million times before. But this time he heard something else, too, something tough and determined that came from much deeper down. *There has to be a way,* it said. *Think.*

He sat back on his heels and studied the ground in front of him. There was no way to get rid of the horrible web of roots. But maybe he could do something different. If the mat was that thick and that tough, maybe he should leave it where it was—and hollow out a space *underneath* it, where the earth was loose. That would leave him with a kind of living, thatched roof over his burrow.

He gave himself a break while he planned it out. Struggling back toward the flattened silk trees, he pulled down some more floss and picked the seeds out of it. While he chewed them, he hunted for something to drink. But there was no sign of a stream and he didn't want to go too far from his burrow. In the end, he pushed his way into the bamboo clumps and sucked at the wet leaves. Then he went back to the digging.

Finishing his burrow seemed like the most important thing in the world. He wanted to be able to crawl safely inside it and block up the door. He wanted to sleep in a shelter of his own. To think, *I made this. I can survive.*

27

That kept him digging, but it was horrible work. The root mat stayed in place above his head, but the soil around the roots crumbled, falling down into his hair and his eyes and his mouth. He closed his eyes and dug blindly, feeling the shape of the space with his fingers.

At first it was just a hollow, big enough to take his hands while he scooped the earth away. After a while he could put his head in. Then his arms and shoulders. Gradually, inch by inch, he excavated a narrow, horizontal tunnel, running along under the roots.

Every ten minutes or so, he had to wriggle out backward and spend time scooping the loose earth and stones out of the hole and onto the surface. Each time, when he went back into the tunnel, he was shocked by how small it was. When he had first made the plan, he had imagined a real underground room. But after an hour or so, he knew that that was beyond him. The most he could aim at was a space big enough to lie down in.

He scrabbled and scraped, crawled in and backed out, time after time. On and on and on. The work seemed to get harder and harder as he grew tired, and the constant rubbing of earth made his hands and knees and elbows dry and sore.

But he kept going. And by the time it was dark, he had done just enough. His original hole had been worn into a ramp, sloping steeply down to the tunnel entrance. The tunnel itself was long enough to take his body, stretched out flat, with a little space all around it. If he went in feet first, the hole wasn't too claustrophobic, and the root mat overhead was easily thick enough to keep out the rain.

It felt like a triumph, but he was too exhausted to celebrate. He just crawled into the burrow and fell asleep.

WHEN HE WOKE UP, HE THOUGHT HE WAS DYING. HIS HEAD throbbed and thudded, and his whole body was stiff and aching as though heavy feet had trodden all over it. He had to force himself to crawl out of the dugout and stand up, and the effort made him retch. Even his skin felt strange. It was thickly smeared with mud that dried and cracked as he moved.

It was very dark. The moon hadn't risen yet, and the leaning tree trunks circled him with shadows. Stumbling out of the circle, he crept back between the bamboo mounds to the loop of creeper where he had hung his fleece. In his exhaustion, after the digging, he'd forgotten all about it. Now he was cold and shivering, and he needed it. He put out a hand to pull it down.

It was soaking wet again. Every thread of it. Drenched.

He'd forgotten about the dew.

A wave of anger hit him, so strong it almost knocked him over. He'd done everything he could. Worked himself into the ground. (*Literally. Ha-ha.* He could almost hear Emma making the joke in her quick, scornful voice.) He had been determined and dogged and persevering—and it was all useless. His body ached from head to foot, crippled with digging and dehydration, and he was still cold and hungry and thirsty.

It's not fair! He wanted a dry fleece and a bottle of water and a heap of cheese sandwiches, and—and—

Without thinking, while he was still raging, he put his hand up to his mouth, to suck off the dampness from the fleece.

It took him a moment to realize that it was water. That he was standing right next to a good store of it. It might not be neat and hygienic, in a plastic bottle, but it was water all the same. The fleece was full of it.

He unhooked it and held it up over his head, wringing it out piece by piece. Without worrying about dirt, or about the dull taste, he let the water fall straight into his mouth, squeezing out as much as he could. Then he sucked at the strands, to make sure he hadn't missed a single drop.

When there was nothing left, he felt his way back to the tree circle and draped the fleece over one of the leaning tree trunks near his burrow. There was no chance of getting it dry again until the sun came up, but at least it would be close at hand.

The water had made him feel a bit better, but he was still thirsty and hungry and aching all over. Fumbling his way out of the circle again, he began to move among the bamboo clumps, searching for something to eat, but it was hopeless. After a couple of steps, he caught his foot on a bamboo root and fell full length. And when he pulled himself up, he took another step—and fell again.

The third time he fell, he understood that he was being stupid. Hunger wasn't going to kill him right away. But if he sprained an ankle or broke a leg, then he would be stuck— and he would certainly starve to death. He had to be patient and wait for the light.

He turned back toward his burrow, walking very cautiously now so that he kept his footing. When he reached the ramp, it felt like coming home. He slithered down backward and landed on his knees, ready to wriggle in, feet first. Dropping onto all fours, he slid one leg back.

And his toes touched fur.

He shot out of the burrow and up the ramp in a single, electric leap. It was an instinctive reaction, way beyond his control. The moment his skin touched the fur, he was out of the burrow and away, and he didn't stop until he reached the first tree.

Then he made himself turn around and listen.

There was no sound.

He listened for a long time. Eventually—when his heart had stopped beating loudly enough to hear—he crept back into the circle, to the heap of earth and stones that had come out of the burrow. Picking up one of the stones, he threw it as hard as he could into the entrance of the tunnel.

Nothing happened.

He threw three more stones before he felt brave enough to go down and investigate. When he did, he inched down the ramp with a stone in each hand, holding his breath as he went.

At the mouth of the tunnel, he stopped to listen again, crouching to peer into the darkness ahead of him. It was still and quiet. The only sound he could hear was the noise of his own breathing. Leaning forward tensely, ready to run away at any moment, he threw a fifth stone into the opening, flinging it as hard as he could.

He heard a clink as it hit one of the other stones. Then— nothing.

Moving infinitely slowly, he put a hand right into the burrow. It touched fur. But the fur wasn't firm and solid. It gave way under his hand, as though there was nothing behind it to give it shape.

Still moving very slowly, he curled his fingers, closing them around a handful of fur and skin. And then—slowly, slowly—he pulled. And pulled again.

It came out easily. It was fur all right, so thick that he could bury his fingers in it. But he couldn't make out its color in the dark, and he had no idea what sort of creatures would live in that strange forest. Grizzly bears? Wolves? Jaguars?

His hands moved across the fur, hauling it right out of the tunnel. It seemed to be a single, flat piece, with a ridge running across the center of it, like a rough seam. Someone had sewn two separate skins together to make a fur blanket.

Some *person* had sewn them together.

And someone had pushed the blanket into his burrow while he was out looking for food.

He knelt with the fur in his hands, listening to the night. Beyond the circle of trees, he could hear rustles and scrapes. There was a strange, deep roar, like the noise of a far-off waterfall. And there were odder sounds, too, noises that he couldn't interpret. But none of the noises sounded human.

He thought about shouting, to attract the attention of whoever it was who had left the fur blanket. *Hello? Are you there? Can anyone hear me? HELLO?*

But he didn't shout.

Instead, he felt around in the burrow, gathering up all the stones he had thrown. Then he wrapped himself in the blanket, with the fur next to his skin, and backed into the tunnel. When he was settled, he piled the stones in a little heap in front of him, where he could reach them easily. He didn't sleep. He lay with his head propped on one hand, looking up the dark ramp. Keeping watch.

5

Cam noticed right away that the bat fur had gone.
It was her job to notice things. The first ripening of the
hedge fruit. Which stores were running low in the cavern. The
best places to pick up wood. Where the ropes needed mending.

There were dozens of things that had to be noticed, every
day, just to keep life going. The others all worked hard, but it
was Cam who knew what had to be done. Wherever she went
she took in scents and sights and sounds and the changing feel
of the air. And she knew every inch of the cavern and what
happened inside it.

That was why she spotted the missing bat fur so quickly.

Lorn had rearranged the other furs, fluffing them up to
make the pile look as tall as ever. It was a good try, but not good
enough. Cam noticed the difference the moment she glanced
into the corner. She didn't say anything, though. Not then.

She waited until the evening, when they were all together,
after the food. She waited until Zak was about to begin a
story, when everyone's attention was focused in the same
place. Then, as Zak reached for his drum, she held up her
hand to stop him.

Standing up she walked over to the pile in the corner and
found her own furs. Without any explanation she came back
to her place in the circle and spread them on the ground in
front of her. Both of them. Then she nodded to indicate that
everyone else should do the same.

They went in turn, fetching the furs and laying them down. Lorn waited until everyone else had moved. Then she stood up slowly and walked across to the corner, where the last fur lay tumbled on the ground. Picking it up, she brought it back to her place in the circle. She didn't sit down. She stood with the fur hanging from her hands in a single sheet.

"Do you want to speak?" said Cam.

Lorn hung her head. "It was the cold," she muttered. "He was very cold."

Cam knew already where the fur had gone. She had guessed it from the first moment. Now she felt the shock of that knowledge go around the cavern as the others took it in. Her eyes flicked from one face to another, assessing their reaction. Working out the best way to deal with it.

Perdew and Ab were visibly angry. They had braved the bat tree to collect the last two furs, and they knew the value of the blankets better than anyone else. For some of the others—like Shang and Tina—the broken rule was the most significant thing, because that threatened their security. And some people—like Nate—had gone very quiet, waiting to see what happened.

Only Bando was unaware of what was going on. He sat playing with a corner of the nearest fur, rubbing his hand backward and forward over the thick, soft surface, as though the whole business had nothing to do with him.

Cam's eyes traveled around the cavern until they reached Zak, who was sitting beside her. He met her eyes, but he didn't react at all. There was no sign to guide her. She had to make this decision on her own.

She made it quickly. Leaving her furs where they were, she

stood up and walked slowly across the circle toward Lorn, aiming straight at her. At the very last moment—exaggerating the gesture so that everyone could see it—she averted her eyes and walked past, so close that she brushed Lorn's shoulder.

One by one the others followed her, walking by in silence, as though Lorn didn't exist. Annet turned her head away, almost in tears, and Nate touched Lorn's hand quickly as he passed, but no one met her eyes. No one spoke. Led by Cam they all made a new circle, farther from the brazier.

Last of all, Zak stood up and took Bando's hand, leading him after the others into the new circle. Bando shuffled past Lorn, muttering wretchedly and turning his head away so hard that the cords stood out on his neck. He and Zak sat down in the last two places, and Zak looked around the circle afresh, catching everyone's attention for the story.

Only Cam looked beyond the circle, toward the red glare of the brazier.

Lorn stood for a moment, waiting for Zak to speak. When he started she knelt down and began to move the furs back into a pile, folding them neatly with her quick, deft hands.

6

FOR TWO DAYS, ROBERT HARDLY LEFT THE CIRCLE OF TREES.

He knew that he ought to explore the whole area. That he should be looking for the wreckage of the plane and hunting for other survivors. But the plane seemed remote and unreal next to the physical warmth of the fur blanket. He couldn't bear the idea of missing another visit from the person who had left that.

So he stayed close to the burrow, trying to find enough food and water to survive.

Water was easy. The strange heavy dew of the first night appeared again on the second evening. And the third. When the sun had gone and the ground around him started to cool, the great, swelling drops of water formed around him, on every leaf edge. He had no way to store it, so he spent large parts of the night drinking, crawling carefully around in the darkness from one leaf clump to another.

Food was more difficult. He had no idea about what was good to eat and what might be poisonous. On the first day after digging the burrow, he had nothing except seeds from the silk tree. He felt safe with those, because he'd eaten them on the first night, when he was dazed and reckless. They hadn't done him any harm, but they weren't enough on their own. The seeds were dry and tough, and their husks caught in his throat if he didn't peel them carefully.

On the second day, he realized that there were big seeds

inside some of the bamboo clumps. A lot of them were moldy, rotting under heaps of wet leaves, but he picked out the good ones and carried them back to his burrow.

They were bigger than the silk seeds and harder. He couldn't crack the husks with his hands or his teeth, but he found a way of smashing them open with stones. The chewing took a long time, and he had to give up before he had eaten them all, because they were so dry. In the end he prepared a heap and kept them until nightfall, when he had water to drink with them.

He ate all he could and then crawled into the burrow to sleep, reminding himself of how lucky he was. He had food and water. He had a dry fleece and a fur blanket. He had survived another day.

But he knew it wasn't good enough. He was only just getting by. The seeds were starting to give him a stomachache, and he couldn't live on them forever.

I have to find some other people. And other kinds of food. I have to get out of here.

Tomorrow.

Tomorrow . . .

THE NEXT DAY, HE SAW SOMETHING MOVING.

It was just starting to get light, and he was sitting on the ground outside the burrow, deciding which way to go to hunt for food. Glancing between the bamboo clumps, he saw a movement in the distance, on the far side of the pale wood.

He jumped up and started forward, peering through the trees. A strange, ungainly shape lumbered across the space between two distant bamboo clumps, moving slowly and steadily. His heart thudded and he stood up abruptly.

It wasn't a big animal. It looked the size of a large dog, but there was nothing doglike about it. It had a coat of armor. The whole of its back was covered with gray plates. They rippled slightly as it clambered over the crawling bamboo stems.

Armadillo, said Robert's brain. He closed his eyes for a second, feeling sick.

When he opened them again, the armadillo had disappeared behind the next clump.

He began to run toward the place where he'd seen it, stumbling and staggering. It was impossible to go fast. His fleece got snagged on the bamboo leaves, and he kept tripping and falling. It took him several minutes to reach the far side of the trees, and when he got there, he could see no sign of the armadillo.

He poked about, peering into one clump after another, but he didn't find anything. He'd been too slow. There were no footprints, no droppings—nothing.

You imagined it, said his brain.

But he knew he hadn't. He was in a forest full of strange creatures living their own lives. Creatures with thick, warm fur. Creatures with armor plating. Creatures that made shrill, piercing noises in the night.

And he ought to be hunting them.

The cold thought slipped into his brain like a slug slithering over a leaf. *I should have caught the armadillo. I should have killed it.*

Instantly he was revolted. Filled with a terrible, longing ache for home. He didn't want to turn into some kind of macho, survivalist hunter. He wanted food that came on a plate and drink that was there whenever he felt thirsty. He wanted a world that was made to fit him, where everything wasn't a gigantic, exhausting effort.

He wanted pepperoni pizza and french fries.

Ice cream and sausages and microwave meals.

Cans of cold Coke.

Even the ordinary, dripping tap in the kitchen seemed like a wonderful, wild dream. *Here's a glass. . . . Put the kettle on for tea, will you?. . . Wash your hands before you slice the bread. . . . I really must change that washer. . . .*

Water torture.

He dragged himself back to the burrow, collecting as many seeds as he could on the way. The thought of eating them nearly choked him, but he couldn't afford to be choosy. He had to eat and drink what he could get.

Sunlight was beginning to filter down through the branches of the pale trees, but he didn't stay to take advantage of it. He carried the seeds down into his burrow, wrapping them close to his body, inside the fur blanket. Then he closed his eyes.

For the first time, he slept not because he was tired, but because he didn't want to think.

WHEN HE WOKE UP AGAIN, IT WAS EVENING. AND THERE WAS a large, round shape at the top of the entrance ramp, blocking out the light.

He waited for a moment, holding his breath and listening. The air was full of mysterious sounds, but they all felt distant, unconnected with the round, dark shape above him. That looked inanimate and unthreatening. Almost reassuring. He stared at it for a moment and then slid out of the blanket and went to investigate.

It was huge—like a beach ball—and its surface was a dull, deep red, with a soft sheen where it caught the evening light. One side was slightly shrunken, as if it had started to dry out, and the top was crowned with a circle of dry, brown fragments sticking up jaggedly.

Was it a fruit? Was it edible?

Scrambling up the ramp, Robert squatted down next to it and prodded it cautiously. It seemed to be covered with a tough skin, so thick that his finger hardly made a dent. Could it be some kind of giant pumpkin?

His body didn't wait for him to figure out the answer. While he was still thinking, his hands started moving over the ground, hunting for something to help them break through that tough skin. The first stone he found was round and blunt, but the second had a sharp edge. In seconds he was pounding at the top of the thing, putting all his weight behind the stone. The skin was strong and leathery, but it didn't take long to puncture it.

As soon as there was a hole, he seized one edge of it and pulled, tugging it taut with one hand and bashing at the stretched skin with the other. A big piece of skin came away in a jagged flap. Pushing his fingers into the flesh underneath, he scooped out a handful and looked at it.

It felt starchy and rather dry—nothing like melon flesh. When he sniffed it, there was no strong smell. Tentatively he lifted his hand to his mouth and ate a piece. It tasted bland and faintly sweet. Not delicious, but sustaining and easy to eat. He finished the rest of that handful and plunged his fingers back into the skin, scooping again.

It was an incredible relief to eat something different from the hard, tough seeds. He scooped and ate and scooped and ate, on and on and on. There was a big stone in the center of the fruit and he worked his way around it, tearing at the skin as he went.

He didn't stop until he had eaten half the fruit. By that time his stomach was uncomfortably full. He lifted his head to see whether there was any dew yet on the clumps beyond the trees.

And he saw a figure duck down quickly, dodging out of sight.

It wasn't an animal this time. It looked like—

He flung himself forward, yelling the first words that came into his head. "Stop! Don't go! You can't go—"

Something brown and agile—something that might, just might, have been a human figure—took off running, darting and ducking between the mounds of bamboo, so that he lost track of it almost immediately.

"Stop!" he shouted again.

He started to run, but before he was out of the circle of trees, the figure had vanished completely.

7

HE THOUGHT ALL NIGHT ABOUT THAT SHADOWY, DARTING figure.

The fur had kept him warm and the starchy fruit had fed him, but he wanted more than occasional gifts from an invisible friend. He wanted to see another human face. He wanted to ask questions and exchange help and share protection.

He wanted to make contact with *people*.

That came first, before everything else. If his elusive benefactor wouldn't stay to meet him, he had to make sure he was ready for the next visit.

He laid his plans carefully, thinking out what he was going to do and then preparing for it. The first thing he needed was a stock of food, so that he could go for two or three days without any distractions. He spent the whole next day amassing that.

He worked his way systematically across the pale wood, gathering all the bamboo seeds that weren't moldy. He stripped the rest of the flesh from the beach-ball fruit and draped the strips on loops of creeper, to dry. Then he climbed the spiraling creeper to collect more fibers from the silk trees, and spent hours picking out the seeds.

In the evening—in case anyone was watching—he made a great show of breaking and eating the seeds he had collected, grinding them between his two stones. But he ate very little. Most of the food was stored inside his burrow, wrapped in the fur blanket.

The next day, he smuggled the food out, handful by handful. He went backward and forward through the pale wood, pretending to look for more supplies. As he went, he trickled handfuls of broken seeds into one of the bamboo clumps. By sunset he had enough for two days stored inside his chosen hiding place.

He was ready to watch.

He went to bed as usual, wrapping himself in the fur and sliding backward into his burrow. But he didn't sleep. He waited for the early darkness, before the moon rose.

His fleece and his body were both stained and dirty by now, and he hoped that would camouflage him as he slid out of the mouth of the tunnel. He arranged the fur blanket behind him, rolling it loosely to give the impression that he was still there. Then he crept up the ramp, moving slowly and keeping close to the ground. Inch by inch he worked his way over the bamboo stems, on his hands and knees, until he reached the clump where he meant to hide.

It was just outside the circle of trees. He wriggled his way in quietly, parting the bamboo and crawling between the stems. In the center, the leaves were soft and damp, and he squirmed around and around, making a space to settle. Peering between the outside leaves, he separated them slightly in two or three places, to make narrow peepholes.

There was no chance of a long view—he was closed in by other clumps all around—but he could see the entrance to his burrow. No one could approach that without being noticed. Crossing his legs he settled back against the bamboo stems, watching.

THE NIGHT PASSED VERY SLOWLY, FULL OF MYSTERIOUS NOISES. There were roars and creaks and deep, harsh sounds that seemed to come at him through the ground. At first he turned his head about, trying to identify each one, but that made the leaves rustle, so he forced himself to keep still, patiently watching the burrow.

By morning he was stiff and cold. He stretched his arms and legs as much as he could, and ate a little of the crushed seed meal. In spite of all his determination to stay awake, he found himself dozing fitfully, starting back to consciousness whenever a sound disturbed him.

Nobody came. The day wore on, slowly, slowly, until he was ready to scream with boredom and frustration. But he made himself stay where he was. He had planned to watch for two days, and he wasn't going to give up.

After a very long time, the light began to die away. The shapes outside lost color, blurring together into teasing, indefinite silhouettes. The grass clumps huddled all around him like hunched animals.

And then the dewdrops started to appear.

Until that happened, he had been resolute. He had intended to stay right in the heart of his clump, waiting for the dew to trickle down to him. But he hadn't counted on seeing so much water so close. Once the moon came out, there were dewdrops hanging just beyond reach, whichever way he peered, and his thirst was more than he could bear. He had to drink. Parting the leaves he started to wriggle free, keeping low and quiet.

And that was when it happened.

As he stopped to unhook his fleece from the leaves, for the fourth or fifth time, he caught a flicker of movement out of the corner of his eye. Someone—*something*—was creeping through the pale trees, toward the entrance of the burrow.

He froze, holding his breath so that he wouldn't frighten it away.

It stepped into the open space inside the circle of trees, and he saw that it was human. That was obvious from the way it moved. But it looked hunched and distorted, with a great lump on its shoulders. It had almost reached the ramp before Robert realized that the lump was a bundle tied high on its back.

At the top of the ramp, it stopped and turned its head from side to side, listening. Robert forced himself to stay motionless. He was outside his hiding place now, relying on shadows and stillness to keep him invisible.

The dark figure listened for a moment longer. Then it squatted down on the far side of the big stone, which was all that was left of the huge red fruit. Sliding the bundle off its back and onto the ground, it bent forward over it.

Robert recognized his chance. Slowly, slowly, he began to crawl toward the circle of trees, listening for every tiny sound that came from the burrow. He heard a faint scraping and then a quick, impatient sigh and the shadowy figure bent lower, almost invisible now behind the fruit stone.

When Robert reached the tree circle, he stopped for a second. Now there was nothing between him and his visitor except a short stretch of open ground covered with bamboo stems. If he was careful, he could cross it in four steps. He took a long breath—slow and silent—and stood up.

Instantly the shadow by the burrow moved, jumping to its feet. For the first time, Robert saw her clearly in the pale light of the moon.

He hadn't been expecting a girl. She was small and slight, with long hair tied back tightly. Her face and body were smeared dark with mud, and she was wearing some kind of short tunic.

While he was still staring, she began to run, moving fast over the tangled ground. She headed away from him, crossing the circle to get to the dark forest.

Robert ran, too, determined not to let her get away, but he never had any real chance of catching her. She was fast and nimble, and she knew how to run over the surface of the bamboo stems without catching her feet. He stumbled after her as best as he could, but by the time he reached the far edge of the tree circle, she had disappeared into the thick shadows under the arching branches. He had no idea which way she had gone.

He stood and swore out loud. Two whole days wasted!

Somewhere at the back of his head, Emma's voice mocked him. He knew exactly what she would have said. *So what is your problem? You've got all the days you want and nothing to do. . . .* But that was wrong. He had everything to do. And he had wasted a whole day—a whole food-gathering, tool-making, exploring day—on something with no result.

Or had he?

When he stumbled back to the entrance of the burrow, he found that the girl had left her bundle behind. It was lying on the ground at the top of the ramp, abandoned in the moonlight. There was a curled leaf that had obviously been rolled up for carrying. Now it was laid out almost flat, and on it was a pile of white crumbs, heaped up carefully.

Squatting down, Robert scooped up a small handful and sniffed at them. They were hard and slightly oily, with a faint, unfamiliar smell. When he touched his tongue to them, they tasted rich and nutty, though he could not have said what kind of nut it was.

Next to the leaf was a heap of something dark, lying crumpled on the ground. He picked up the largest piece and examined it, turning it so that the light fell on its surface. It was soft like cloth, but not cloth. Some kind of leather, maybe? The piece he was holding was a large rectangle and underneath it were four cords, made of the same stuff but plaited together for strength.

He guessed that he was holding the makings of the girl's backpack. It was very simple, but the pieces were beautifully made. The leather was fine and soft, and the strings had been plaited evenly. Running his hands over them, Robert tried to figure out how to fit the pack together, but he was too tired to experiment.

He ate a little of the nut stuff and drank some dew, and then he wrapped up the whole bundle in the leather rectangle and carried it down the ramp into his burrow.

It took him several minutes to rearrange the blanket as he wanted it. When that was done, he crawled into the tunnel and slept, with the leather bundle of crushed nuts lodged safely inside the fur, against his back.

8

HE WOKE UP BECAUSE THE LEATHER BUNDLE MOVED.

It slid against his skin and he woke suddenly, rigid with shock. The air was stifling, and the tunnel was pitch-black. In front of his eyes, in the tunnel entrance, he was aware of a solid shape, blocking out the moonlight.

Some instinct kept him utterly still, breathing lightly, as if he were still asleep. After a few moments, he was aware of the darkness . . . shifting. There was no more light than before, but the air quivered, and the hunched shape moved just a fraction closer to his face. He could feel his own breath reflected back against his skin.

The leather bundle slid again, inching along his back toward the entrance.

It was level with his shoulder now, sinking into the angle of his neck. He waited, still pretending to be asleep, ready to react the instant it moved again. There was a long pause. Then the leather slipped another inch—and he rolled over and grabbed, all in one movement.

He was aiming not for the bundle itself, but for the hand that had to be there. His fingers shot forward and closed around a small, bony wrist, so narrow that it almost slipped out of his grasp. He tightened his fingers and brought his other hand around, clamping it over the first one and clinging on with all his strength.

There was a short, fierce struggle in the darkness. The

intruder's other hand darted into the burrow, jabbing at his hands and his face. He closed his eyes tightly and ignored the blows, just concentrating on hanging on. Then his opponent began to strain backward, struggling to tug the arm free.

Robert had no reason to hold his ground. He didn't relax his grip, but he let himself be pulled forward, out of the burrow and up onto the ramp. Once he was out there, he knew who it was that he'd caught. He recognized the shape of the head, with the long hair pulled back from the face.

"I'm a friend—" he said. He was panting with the effort of holding on, but he tried to sound gentle. "I'm . . . a friend. Don't be afraid."

There was no reason for her to understand the actual words, but he hoped that the tone of his voice would reassure her. And it seemed to have some effect. She stopped struggling and lay back against the ramp, looking up at him with eyes that glinted in the moonlight. Not afraid, but watchful.

Keeping his fingers tightly clamped, he leaned forward and spoke again. "I'm a friend. I need help. I think my plane crashed."

She understood the words.

He saw her understand. It was very quick—a brief flash of attention—but there was no mistaking it. She had understood him. He was so startled—so relieved and amazed—that his fingers loosened involuntarily.

Immediately the girl moved, pulling her hand free and darting out of his grasp. Robert lunged forward, expecting her to race up the ramp. But she dodged around him, heading back into the tunnel, and he almost sprawled headlong.

Just in time he realized what she was up to. He threw himself back, not caring how he fell, but desperate to snatch up the bundle before she reached it. Their hands clashed, and he flung his arm out sideways, pushing her away.

He hadn't realized how light she was. His blow threw her off balance completely, knocking her off her feet. He caught at the long tail of her hair, winding his fingers into it and tugging her head down to the ground.

Then he slid his other hand around behind him, feeling for the leather bundle. His brain was whirling, trying to think of how to use what had happened. He didn't understand what the girl was up to, but she might be one of the survivors from the plane crash. If she was, she might know where the others were, or where the wreckage had landed.

He scrambled onto his knees and pulled her head up, leaning forward to look into her face. "Right," he said softly. "This is what we're going to do. You want this backpack, don't you?"

He shook it in the air, just out of her reach. She twisted her head sideways to look up at it, but he couldn't see her expression.

"Let's make a bargain." He shook the backpack again. "You want this—and I want to see where you live. I want to meet the other people."

There was no response, but he could feel her listening— and he knew he had to get it right. He pulled her back to face him and went on talking, with his brain going at lightning speed.

"I'm going to let go of your hair in a minute. You'll be able to run away if you want to. But make sure I can follow you. You won't get this pack until I see where you live."

There was a long silence. Robert was hoping for an answer, but she didn't say anything. She just waited to run, with all her muscles tensed, ready to leap up. He had to take the gamble and let her go. If the backpack was really precious to her, she would let him follow.

"OK," he said. And he slid his fingers out of her hair.

The moment he let go, she lunged forward, trying to snatch the backpack while he was still kneeling. But before she could touch it, he was on his feet, holding it high above her head.

"No chance," he said. "There's only one way you'll get this."

She drew in her breath with an angry hiss. Then she jumped up and ran, racing up the ramp and across the circle of trees, toward the dark forest. Robert tore up the ramp after her, but he thought he'd blown it. There was no way he could match her speed over the bamboo stems.

She obviously realized that. When she reached the edge of the dark trees, she turned and looked over her shoulder to check that he was following. She hovered for a moment, until he was well on the way, and then set off again, moving just fast enough to keep a safe distance ahead.

Robert had never trailed anyone before. When he had given the instructions, he had imagined himself gliding after her like a snake, soundless and unseen. He had visualized himself covering the ground easily, with his eyes fixed on the fleeing shape in front of him.

The truth was laughably different. Every step he took was a separate effort. He had to watch where he put his feet and keep an eye out for low branches overhead. His feet slipped and squelched on the wet leaves, and where the earth was bare he had to scramble over heavy clods and big, irregular boulders.

The leather bundle hampered him, because it left him with only one free hand. But he couldn't ditch it. The girl kept glancing back, to check that it was still there. If she saw him without it, he would lose sight of her instantly. He had no illusions about that. She was twice as fast as he was, as though she had some kind of extra sense that lit up the darkness. He could see her twisting and turning along paths that were virtually invisible to him.

Gradually she led him deep into the forest, and it grew thicker and more tangled. A dank, foul-smelling creeper wove its way in and out of the great splayed tree trunks, blocking the way with its vast leaves. Robert found himself ducking around them and squeezing through narrow spaces, and he began to wonder if he was being led into a trap.

Then, just as it seemed as if they were reaching the dense heart of the jungle, the forest opened out again. The huge, looping trunks gave way to shorter trees and thick, green bushes. Stepping carefully through these, the girl led him out into a patch of moonlight.

They were standing on the edge of a long, deep ravine.

It ran left and right as far as Robert could see, disappearing into the darkness in both directions. Its walls went down sheer and vertical, thick with vegetation, and the bottom was hidden in dense shadow. On the far side, a great wall of forest reared up like a rampart, hiding the sky.

The girl turned and began to race along the side of the ravine, moving very fast now. She seemed to know every stone and every crack in the earth, and Robert had no chance of keeping up. He struggled on, just managing to keep her in sight.

Until—quite suddenly—she vanished.

She had been heading for a place where the ravine was bridged by a fallen tree. The trunk lay right across, from bank to bank, with the branches holding the nearer end off the ground. The girl ran around the spreading branches and disappeared. And the sound of her feet stopped abruptly.

Robert felt his heart thud. Was this it? Had they reached the other survivors? Was the crashed plane down there at the bottom of the ravine?

Or was this a trick?

He slowed down, moving warily and keeping the leather bundle clutched close to his chest. The tree was an ideal place for an ambush. He gave the dead branches a wide berth, trying to peer in underneath them as he crept past.

Nothing moved. On the other side of the tree, there was no sign of the girl. The forest around him was silent except for its usual strange creaks and rumbles. Cautiously, he took another step, away from the fallen trunk.

And a hand snaked out of the ravine and caught him around the ankle, pulling him to the ground.

Before he could yell, the girl's other hand lay over his mouth and her face was close to his. She shook her head hard, hushing him fiercely. Then she reached for the bundle.

They were poised on the very edge of the ravine, above what looked like a bottomless gulf. The girl was wedged into a clump of bushes, but there was nothing below Robert except a sheer drop. He was terrified.

But he wasn't going to be bullied.

He lifted the bundle out of her reach and jerked his head free. "Not good enough," he whispered fiercely. "Where are the others?"

The girl made impatient movements with her hand, hushing him again. Then she pointed across the ravine. Robert felt like shaking her.

"Why don't you *speak*?"

She shook her head and reached up again for the bundle.

It looked like the end of bargaining. She was obviously frightened, and she kept glancing nervously across the ravine. Robert could feel her resistance, like something solid between them. She obviously didn't want to lose the backpack, but there was some other threat hanging over her. Something much bigger.

His only chance now was to take another gamble.

He lowered his arm and dropped the bundle into the girl's hand. She grabbed it and hauled herself up the slope in a single, fluid movement. By the time Robert was on his feet, she had already scrambled into the crown of the fallen tree.

He saw her running out along the trunk, perfectly balanced and very fast. Desperate to keep her in sight, he threw himself at the branches, but they were sharp and bent at awkward angles. It wasn't easy to climb up onto the trunk. By the time he had pulled himself up, the girl had disappeared again.

He stepped out onto the trunk and stood still, listening. After a moment or two, he thought he could make out the sound of voices, faint and muffled, coming from the other side of the ravine. He began to walk along the trunk, keeping his mind focused on the noise.

The tree trunk was broad and solid, easily wide enough for a bridge, but it wasn't smooth. Long ridges ran from end to end, and the surface bristled with curious, stiff hairs that spiked his shins. There was a path worn through the bristles, but it was hard to follow, and he had to pick his way carefully.

He was halfway along when he was plunged into darkness.

Overhead, a vast shadow blocked out the moonlight. He flung his head back, looking up, and saw a great, black shape coming at him from above. It fell through the air, too fast to escape, blotting out the whole sky.

But it can't be. . . .

There was no sound. Only the wind in his ear and on the back of his neck, and a nightmare heading straight for him, too big to understand.

9

I<small>T WAS BEYOND COMPREHENSION, CRACKING THE WORLD WIDE</small> open. His brain refused to grasp it. Reality shattered into a hurricane of senseless, appalling images.

A glaring, gelatinous globe gleamed black and yellow, as big as his whole body. Claws reached out toward him like the arms of a great machine, ingrained with earth and blood. Vast, ribbed pinions beat up a hurricane of stinking air, foul with decay.

Anything was better than that horror—the gulf below him, physical pain, even death. Without hesitating, without even thinking, Robert threw himself sideways, off the bridge, into the black depths of the ravine.

He wasn't fast enough. As his feet left the bridge, the cruel claws screamed down onto it, snapping together and crushing it into fragments. They caught his right thigh, slicing through the flesh and clamping the bone.

Screaming with pain and fear, Robert was hoisted into the air, with his whole weight dangling from one tortured leg. Huge wings beat around him. The air sucked and swirled over his body, and as it swung he felt the flesh tear and he started to black out.

Blindly he reached up, twisting his body double, with all his muscles straining as he searched for something to hold. His hands moved over the hard claw that dug into his leg and found a tough, feathery fringe above it. Winding his fingers into the strands of feather, he heaved himself up, taking the weight off his tortured thigh.

The great wings steadied, banking and turning, rising up out of the forest, above the tops of the trees. Up and up and up. Robert's stomach lurched, and he retched, jerking at his wound as his body convulsed.

There was another turn and another vicious, excruciating swing. For a moment he was hovering in midair, with nothing below him except thick darkness and an unimaginable drop. Then they spun away again, sideways and down, and landed with a lurch.

Robert was slammed onto a hard surface, so violently that he lost his hold. The claws still gripped him tightly, but the rest of his body was flung backward, arms sprawling. The fierce, yellow eyes came roaring at him, huge and alien. Below them was a gigantic, murderous hook, aiming straight at his belly.

Beyond thought—beyond everything—he scrabbled backward, scraping his outflung arms over the roughness under him. His fingers closed over something long and straight, and he snatched at it, bringing it around and up in one fast, violent movement.

The fierce eyes were so close that the nearest one filled his whole field of vision. He jabbed straight at it with his weapon, as hard as he could. Into the black, gleaming center.

There was a furious screech. The hooked beak recoiled for an instant. Then it stabbed back at him, and this time he didn't escape completely. As he went for the other eye, the beak ripped at his arm, opening a long, jagged wound. But he hardly felt the pain. He continued to strike into the soft tissue around the eye.

The creature flinched and released its claw for a split second. That was enough. Robert rolled away, as fast as he could, without worrying where he might land. His raw flesh scraped over rough, serrated ridges—and plunged into emptiness.

All around him there was nothing except space. He was falling down and down and down into darkness.

For a long, terrifying moment, he thought that he was falling the whole dizzying distance back down to the ground, to smash through the tree-trunk bridge and into the gulf below. But then the air thickened, chokingly, and he understood that he was somewhere inside, falling deeper and deeper in.

As he grasped that, he hit the bottom, plunging into a soft litter of rotting wood. He was in a dark, close space that reeked of blood and death.

He retched once more, and then the darkness slid inside his head, and he passed out.

HE CAME TO GRADUALLY, DRAGGING HIMSELF OUT OF unconsciousness, taking a long time to focus.

There was a dim light now, coming from somewhere way above his head. Images formed and blurred and formed again as he lay looking up, turning his head slowly to take everything in.

He was lying in an ogre's den.

It was a tall, grim cavern, roughly circular, with ragged, ribbed walls. There was a stench of rotten meat. The light—what there was of it—came from two small openings, high in one of the walls, and it shone down on a litter of old bones, some of them still carrying shreds of flesh.

Robert felt sick and dazed, but he knew that he had to get

away from that place. His wounds had stopped bleeding, but they ached and throbbed, and the idea of infection terrified him. Already he felt too weak to fight, and if he went on lying in that filthy den he would get worse. If the nightmare ogre-bird didn't come to get him, he would die of blood poisoning.

He had to get out, but there was no easy way to escape. The only openings were high above his head. To reach them he would have to climb up the walls of the cavern, almost to the top. Was that possible?

He moved, experimentally.

His right leg was stiff and awkward, but there was none of the agony he was expecting. The leg seemed to have gone numb. He wasn't sure how much blood he had lost. There were dark stains underneath him, but the dust had caked his wound, forming a crust that had sealed it and stopped the bleeding.

The wound on his arm was much more painful. He poked at it with his other hand. It wasn't deep, and it didn't seem to be infected—yet. It hurt when he moved his arm, but at least he could still do that. The only sensible thing was to grit his teeth and try to climb before it became impossible.

He struggled onto his hands and knees and crawled through the wood dust to the cavern wall. The moment he touched that, he knew that it was wood, too. The cavern was as high as a cathedral, and the whole crumbling, tattered space was lined with rotting wood.

As it had crumbled, the wood had left hundreds of spikes and steps and ledges all the way up the wall. Robert gripped the nearest projection, using it to pull himself up. He was half-expecting it to give way under his weight, but it held firm, and he reached up for the next ledge, feeling around for a foothold with his good leg.

As he hauled himself onto it, his bad leg began to tremble. He pulled it up beside the good one and moved his hands higher. He had to put his weight on the bad leg so that he could find a second foothold. When he had heaved himself onto it, he lay against the wall, recovering from the effort.

He was off the ground. And if he had climbed one step, he could climb another. And another. He gripped one of his wooden handholds and reached for the next.

It took ten times as long as he expected to climb up to the nearest opening, and he had to force himself to concentrate on what he was doing. Each time he rested, he looked up at the opening, afraid that he might see the light blocked out by the terrible silhouette of the ogre-bird. But the light stayed steady. And slowly, as he climbed, it grew brighter and pinker, lighting the wood around it.

From beyond the opening, he could hear unfamiliar noises, but he closed his mind, refusing to wonder about them. His business was climbing, not imagining. And the climbing needed every ounce of will and energy that he could raise.

Just below the opening, he stopped for a long time, gathering his strength. Then he gripped the edge of the hole and hauled himself up, so that his face was level with it. The sudden light dazzled him, and he lowered his forehead onto the wood at the edge of the hole, waiting for his eyes to recover. Breathing the fresh, cold air that was like water running off a mountain.

When he lifted his head again, he could see the rough gray surface outside the hole. It sloped gently upward, falling away at the sides. Heaving himself higher, he wriggled his shoulders through the opening and hauled the rest of his body after them. Once he was out, he sprawled full length for a couple of minutes, exhausted and shaking. Then he rolled over and sat up cautiously.

He was sitting in some kind of gigantic tree, vast beyond anything he had ever seen or imagined. The branch where he sat was as wide as a room, with rutted, irregular bark, covered with grotesque swellings. Leaves stretched over his head like awnings and clustered underneath him, shutting out most of the view in all directions.

But straight ahead there was a small break in the leaves. By tilting his head slightly, he could see through the break and away into the distance. The view was quite different from anything he had expected.

He was looking down on an expanse of grass as green and level as a lawn. And beyond the grass—

He lifted his eyes and saw a tall red spire, rising steadily into the sky.

That's the cathedral, he thought. Automatically.

And then, *It can't be. . . .*

But it was. There was no mistaking the grimy, sandstone ribs, blurred smooth by centuries of weather. He'd known that sight all his life. He could walk there from home in twenty minutes or so.

How could he see the cathedral from this jungle of alien trees and armadillos and monstrous, murderous birds?

He shuffled along the branch, to get a better view. Now he could see the high-rise office buildings in the city center. And the tight sweep of the highway. And the big, new shops, surrounded by seas of empty parking lots. If he looked nearer, he could see his own house, facing him across the expanse of grass.

But looking nearer still—there was a rift in reality.

On the far side of the rift was his home, the ordinary, everyday city where he lived when he wasn't away on vacation or getting involved in plane crashes.

On his side of the rift was the jungle, and the ogre-bird, and the great tree where he was sitting, on the edge of the dark wood.

His eyes moved backward and forward, from one to the other, as he tried to make sense of what he was seeing. Where did one reality end and the other begin?

He looked back at the cathedral and forced himself to put it together. Fixing his eyes on the spire, he slowly let them travel nearer.

Across the city.

Over the highway and the shops.

Past his own house and across the road in front of it, into the park.

Then, slowly, carefully, right across the park, coming nearer and nearer until he saw the hedge in front of the brambly woods

and—looking straight down now—

the normal, ordinary, middle-sized

oak tree

where

he

was

sitting.

———

He did it three times, to make sure. There was no mistake. There was no rift in reality. He was exactly where he seemed to be, sitting in an oak tree on the west edge of the park.

He knew after the first time that it was the only explanation. Even before he turned right and saw the railway line running down the side of the park. But he had to do it three times to make himself take it in.

To understand how far from home he really was.

II

The Cavern

10

KIU, CALLED THE NIGHT BIRD, LOW AND VERY CLOSE. *KIUUUUU.*

In the cavern, Cam looked left and right, counting heads. They were all there, except for Nate and Perdew, and she had no worries about them. They were quick and cunning. No prey for the bird. Everything looked fine.

But her instincts told her there was something wrong. And the bird was part of it.

Lorn knew what was up. That was as plain as the moon on a clear night. Two or three minutes ago she had come crawling in through the tunnel, scrambling as fast as she could. All the others had turned their heads away, looking past her, but Cam had kept watching, surreptitiously. She had seen Lorn's white, breathless face and the empty batpack crumpled in her right hand.

And she'd seen her wince, the first time the night bird called.

Now Lorn was sitting in a corner, away from everyone else. Her head was bent over the batpack, but she wasn't mending it or folding it. Her hands were still. Secretly, under her eyelids, she was staring at the tunnel entrance.

Cam's head was full of questions, but she didn't ask them. She kept her mouth shut and her head turned away. Lorn's punishment wasn't nearly over yet.

The bird called again—*kiuuuuuu*—and there was a scream. Very close to the cavern. It was impossible to tell what creature had made the noise, but it had an unnerving, human sound. Cam heard a rustle as Lorn shifted uneasily, and she saw her shadow flicker on the opposite wall of the cavern.

Bando heard the bird's call, too. He lurched up from beside the brazier, heavy and distraught, with his fists clenched and his great arm muscles knotted.

"The bird's got them," he said, panicky and fearful. "It's got Nate and Perdew."

Cam put a hand on his arm. She could feel him shaking, and she knew what he wanted. He was longing to sidle across to Lorn and bury his head in her shoulder, to let her reassure him. But he knew better than that.

Cam patted the arm as gently as she could. "They're fine," she said. "Don't worry."

But Bando went on trembling.

Kiuuu. The bird was rising into the air now, banking toward the bitter-nut tree. Picturing the flight in her mind, Cam watched Lorn out of the corner of her eye. She saw her head swivel slowly, following the melancholy, drawn-out sound.

There was something wrong, and the bird was part of it.

THE OTHER TWO DIDN'T COME BACK UNTIL IT WAS LIGHT. CAM slept uneasily, listening for them. Just after sunrise, she was woken by noises in the tunnel. Zak was already awake, sitting up in his sleeping place by the entrance. He pulled away the branches that blocked the mouth of the tunnel.

Without turning, Cam heard Lorn sit up, too.

Nate crawled into the cavern slowly, looking very tired, with Perdew close behind him. Without a word Cam went to the shells and fetched them some water. They sat against the wall and drank in turn. Then Perdew leaned back and took a long, shuddering breath.

"He was on the bridge," he said. "Right in the middle, in the open. He *stopped*."

Cam imagined it so sharply that she almost cried out. She saw the small figure standing clear and stark on the fallen trunk. The great wings swooping down. Cruel talons slicing into living flesh. And then—

She turned away abruptly—and bumped into Lorn who had crept up behind her without making a sound. The shock of finding her there sparked Cam into a fury.

"You're a fool!" she said savagely, straight into Lorn's face. The rules didn't matter now. This went way beyond the punishment they'd fixed so far. "I thought we'd warned you enough, but you didn't leave him alone, did you? You led him here. And now you've killed him."

"Killed?" said Bando's voice, quick and fearful, from halfway down the cavern.

Cam hadn't realized that he was awake. They were all waking now. Stirring and muttering, asking each other what had happened. Tina tried to put an arm around Bando's shoulders, but he shook himself free, gazing at Cam and Lorn.

"Lorn's killed someone?" he said.

"Not just me!" Lorn was furious, too, but it was a desperate, unfocused anger, lashing out at everyone. "We all killed him! He didn't know it was dangerous to stop on the bridge. He didn't know *anything!*" It was the first time she had spoken for days, and her voice was raw and harsh. "If we'd told him where he really was—if he'd understood what—"

All across the cavern, people shifted unhappily, muttering in the shadows. Cam spoke quickly, to change the mood.

"He had to prove himself first," she said. "That's how we do it. You know we can't take in everyone. We can't cope—"

We can't cope with any more losers. She couldn't say it, because Bando was there, but they all knew what she meant.

"So we waited," Lorn said bitterly. "And now he's dead."

Nate hesitated. "He might not—"

Suddenly the whole cavern was very still. Perdew looked around and shook his head, but Nate wouldn't be silenced.

"We can't be sure he's dead," he said. "We couldn't see clearly. The night bird had him in its foot, and he twisted as they went up. He must have been alive then—when it took him up into the bitter-nut tree. After that we lost them. We stayed and watched as long as we could, but it was impossible—"

Annet pushed another log onto the brazier, and the fire flared up. In the red light, Cam saw Zak's face sharpen.

"From up in that tree, you can see everything," he said softly.

Cam's mind began to make the picture, and she shut it down fast. "He's not going to see anything, is he?" she snapped. "Not if he's dead."

"But if he's alive—" Zak let the words trail away. There was no need to finish. They all understood what he meant. *If he's alive—he knows now.*

Cam felt her breath stop as the memory came at her. The moment of knowing. It was the memory she'd been holding back—that they'd all been holding back—ever since they'd seen the boy fall out of the sky.

Be careful, Zak, she thought. *Be careful.*

But Zak was never careful. He would say what he had to say. And if they didn't like it, he would disappear, slipping out of the cavern and up into the tangled branches, too fast for anyone to follow. Once he'd been gone for a whole month, and they'd had to tell their own stories, stumbling awkwardly over the words and drawing in the air with their hands.

"Remember how it was," he said, "when you first understood."

Cam wasn't sure she could stand it. "The boy's *dead,*" she said roughly. "You don't have to do this, Zak. Nate and Perdew saw the bird take him."

Zak ignored her. Slowly, with ceremony, he sat down on the ground, crossing his legs and dropping his hands loosely into his lap. One by one the others sat, too, turning to look at him. Waiting for the story.

When everyone was sitting, except for the two by the brazier, Zak began to speak.

"Once there was a girl who lived in a tall tower. Her father was a great wizard, and her mother could change the shapes of things. They conjured a steel tower out of the common earth and used their knowledge and their skills to raise it high into the air, above attack and hunger, above disease and death. It was impregnable."

The cavern stilled. In the shadows, people settled back against the walls, watching Zak's face. Lorn and Dess and Annet. Nate and Perdew. Even Bando in his dark corner.

Even Cam.

"The girl's parents loved her so much," Zak said, "that they shielded her eyes with dark glasses and protected her hands with gloves. They wrapped the tower in spells to keep out

71

grief and pain, and they filled her days with all kinds of magic delights, so that she never needed to leave the tower." He stopped.

"And then?" Dess said, after a moment.

Zak spread his hands. "That's the end. She lived happily ever after."

"But she must have come out of the tower," said Nate.

"Why?" Zak shook his head. "The tower had everything she could possibly need. Why would she want to come down onto the dirty, dangerous ground?"

He looked at Cam, challenging her, but she wouldn't meet his eyes. Nor would Dess or Perdew or Annet or . . . Zak looked at each of them, one by one. No one said a word.

Until he reached Lorn.

Lorn was following his eyes as he turned. When he looked at her, she spoke abruptly. Fiercely. "She has to get out of there. Or she'll die."

"But she has everything she needs," Zak said softly. "Why would she die?"

Lorn stared at him, lost for an answer, and Bando interrupted.

"She has to leave the tower. Or else it's not a story. She has to leave the tower and have adventures."

"What kind of adventure do you want?" Zak said easily. "Shall I make her climb mountains? Wade through rivers? Fight huge monsters?"

"Yes." Bando looked around for support. "That's what happens in stories, isn't it? People go away to have adventures—and at the end they go home again."

The air was so tense that Cam could hardly breathe. She

saw Nate's hands clench into fists and felt her own fingers curl tightly, digging into the palms of her hands.

"But suppose that going home is the *beginning* of the adventure?" Zak said softly. "Suppose the girl goes back to the tower and finds she can't reach the handle?"

He raised his two hands, shaping the solid sides of the tower. Uncoiling as he lifted them, he rose first onto his knees and then onto his feet in a single fluid movement, stretching up and up, with his head tilted right back, staring at something way beyond his reach.

Cam saw the tower rising in front of her, gleaming and unattainable in the firelight. Going up and up and up. To kill the pain, she turned roughly to Lorn, speaking very fast, out of somewhere deeper than reason.

"The boy . . . if he's not dead . . . if he survives . . . he can come into the cavern."

Lorn's head snapped around. She was caught off guard, pulled out of the story, but she was still quick-witted.

"He'll be injured," she said. "Maybe crippled for life."

Cam thought of the bird's quick beak. Of its silent wings and strong, murderous claws. Then she thought of the view from the top of the bitter-nut tree.

"He can come," she said. "Whatever state he's in."

11

WHAT'S THE WORST THING THAT COULD HAPPEN?

Sitting high in the oak tree, Robert could almost hear Emma's voice prodding at him. It was one of her favorite questions. *Is that the worst you can think of?* And he would rack his brains to imagine horrible mutilations and disasters, as though guessing the worst in advance could stop it from happening.

Suppose you went completely blind? Or deaf? Or suppose you lost all your arms and legs? Emma usually went for physical things, and he'd copied her, pretending he'd felt the same. But he'd always known there were worse horrors for him. Things inside his head that would catch him up in a swirl of rushing darkness. *Black terror. Being overwhelmed. Being unmade—* None of the words he could think of got anywhere near.

It had never occurred to him that *the worst* would be something that affected everything. Not just his mind or his body, but the whole world in which he moved. Everything changed and lost—and black terror flooding into the void.

HE SAT IN THE TREE FOR A LONG TIME. NOT MOVING. NOT thinking. Not able to do anything except stare out at the impossible world around him.

The branches made a clear-cut pattern against the light. A pattern with a double meaning.

Flick—and it was a network of twigs, with the old leaves

tarnished and next year's buds already beginning to swell.

Flick—and the same thing became a cage of heavy wood, where the buds were bigger than his fist and the smallest twig was too strong for him to move.

Flick. He was sitting on an ordinary oak branch that stretched up and away in front of him.

Flick. He was stranded on a wide, cambered surface, split with cracks like ground destroyed by drought.

Flick.

His muscles ached. His torn arm hurt. The wound in his leg was red and hot. But his mind floated free and light, making pictures in the air.

The old questions seemed ludicrously simple now. *Where am I? What's going to happen?* He could think about those. But the new ones danced high above his head, right out of reach. How had he ended up so close to home—and so far away? And why? When he started to ask those questions, his brain swerved aside, like a horse at an impossible jump. Words like *delusion* and *hallucination* drifted in and out of his head, but they couldn't link the last moment in the plane and the first moment in the dark wood.

The two realities wouldn't fit together.

IT WAS THIRST THAT FINALLY GOT HIM MOVING. HUNGER WAS nothing. Hunger was a pain he could bear. But by midday, when the sun was high in the sky, his thirst was unendurable.

It was a sick joke. He was tormented by hunger and thirst, in sight of his own house. From where he was, he could actually glimpse the roof of the kitchen. Under that roof, the fridge was crammed with food. There was water on tap. The cupboards were bursting with pasta and rice and cans of beans. One of those cans would keep him alive for a week.

Except that he wouldn't be able to open it.

He pictured himself scuttling across the kitchen floor and scrabbling helplessly at the bottom of the cupboards. Like a tiny cartoon figure, he stood marooned and helpless on the floor while water gushed out of the tap and into the sink.

Pathetic.

Fiercely he shook his head, to get rid of the images. They were no use to him. He had to focus. His only hope of survival was to find the girl he'd seen and join up with her group—whoever they were. He had to find her.

And that meant that he had to climb down the tree.

The black terror surged up in his mind again, but he pushed it back. If he let himself despair, he was dead. He had to be practical. He knew he was sitting in one of the oak trees on the far side of the park. OK. So how tall were those trees? Thirty feet? Fifty? And how tall was he?

He thought about it. To him—as he was now—the tree was like a mountain. It was monstrously high. But he'd climbed mountains before, and going down was usually the easy part. If he started right away, he ought to be on the ground in a couple of hours.

Cautiously he stood up, leaning against the tree trunk with his good arm. He was waiting for pain to knock him side-ways, but it didn't come. His injured leg was numb and wooden. When he took a step away from the trunk, his head swam and he staggered slightly, but it was possible to move.

At the moment.

He wasn't stupid enough to think that the numbness

would last forever. Sometime soon there would be weakness and fever and excruciating pain. He had to get out of the tree before that happened, or he would never do it.

Looking over the side of the branch, he studied the grooved bark of the trunk below him. He had always thought of bark as flat and smooth, but now he saw that this bark was full of ridges and cracks where he could wedge his hands and feet. The ground was terrifyingly far away, but he had learned already that one step after another would take him where he needed to go. If he could climb down at all, then he could make it.

It was still half an hour before he could bring himself to trust his wounded leg and climb off the branch. In the end, the only thing that got him moving was fear of the ogre-bird. If it came back while he was sitting on the branch, he was done for.

Shutting everything else out of his mind, he let himself slowly off the branch and began to climb down the tree trunk.

HE WAS HOPELESSLY WRONG ABOUT THE TIME IT WOULD TAKE. It wasn't at all like walking on a mountain. It was more like inching down a vertical rock face over an abyss, without a rope or an ax to secure him. The holds were good, but he had to concentrate fiercely every second he was climbing—even though his wounded arm ached and his leg trembled unpredictably. It took every ounce of strength and determination he could drag up.

Whenever he reached a branch, he stopped and sprawled out, completely exhausted. But he didn't relax. His eyes moved constantly, watching the sky around him and the endless, complex network of branches.

He was in danger all the time. Every shadow overhead might be a bird that could swoop down and snap him up. Every movement on the ground might be a sharp-toothed creature waiting for him to climb down into its jaws. And he had no weapons and no way of fighting back.

The fear got him climbing again as soon as he could manage it. He stayed alert, freezing whenever he heard a sound or felt a breeze on his cheek, but there was no space for feelings. All his attention was focused on finding the next handhold, the next foothold.

Slowly, slowly he inched down the tree, glad of the mud and dirt and wood dust that covered his body and the filthy fleece that disguised his shape.

Halfway down, he reached a small branch growing at a sharp angle. Settling himself into the crook, he peered at the ground below him, trying to see the bridge where the ogre-bird had snatched him. If he was going to find the strange girl again, he had to get back to that place.

It took him a long time to figure it out. From halfway up the tree, his eyes saw familiar shapes, and his brain named them in the old way. *Park. Hedge. Ditch. Brambly wood.* In that sense, he knew exactly where he was.

The oak tree was growing in the hedge that separated the playing fields from the wood at the far end of the park. Just inside the wood there was a small drainage ditch, running along the back of the hedge.

That's where I was. That's the ravine.

He had to force himself to see it like that. The picture flicked backward and forward unstably in his head, and he had to scan the ditch—the *ravine*—a dozen times before he

78

picked out the dry, broken stalk lying half in and half out of it.

The bridge the ogre-bird had snapped.

From where he was, it looked tiny, like a thread. He understood then how much farther he had to climb, and he put his head down on the branch in front of him and despaired.

He gave up twice more before he reached the bottom of the tree. Once when the wound on his leg broke open and began to bleed. And once when he lost his grip and fell, sliding and crashing through the leaves to land, sore and winded, on a lower branch.

Each time, he lay flat out, utterly wretched. And each time he began to climb again in the end. What else could he do? He had no choice but to keep moving, down and down and down, with his head spinning and his body crying out with pain and exhaustion. Down and down. Down and down and down.

When he reached the bottom, he was too tired to think. Too tired even to worry about the slow leak of blood from his wounds. Instinctively, like any other small, desperate creature, he burrowed into the litter of dry leaves at the foot of the tree. And as soon as he was completely hidden, he fell asleep.

When he woke up, it was pitch-dark and everything was covered with dew. He drank and drank, not caring where the dewdrops were hanging. Then he hauled himself out of the leaves and limped unsteadily down to the edge of the ravine.

He was on the other side now, where the girl had disappeared the night before. The bank of the ravine was thick with tangled plants, and he began to work his way through them, toward the bridge. It was like struggling through a jungle. His leg was heavy and throbbing now, and it was all he could do to stay on his feet. He had to stop and rest every few steps, and by the time he reached the bridge he was light-headed and stumbling.

And he had no idea where to go next.

The girl had run across the bridge, to the place where he was standing now, and then she had vanished. He stood by the broken bridge, swaying and dazed, trying to think of how to find her. There must be . . . clues. A logical way to investigate. There had to be—

But he was beyond thought. He didn't even care whether the people he was hunting for were friendly or hostile. It didn't matter anymore. He just wanted *people*.

Sliding to the ground, in the shadow of the bridge, he lifted his voice and shouted, with all the energy he had left.

"Help! Help me! Where are you?"

The words echoed horribly in his head. An idiot's trumpeting. *Here I am! Come and kill me!* Above him and all around, the deep sounds of the night rumbled and creaked incomprehensibly. *Here I am! Come and kill me!* He didn't dare to shout again. Shrinking deeper into the shadows, he waited to see what would happen.

THREE OF THEM CAME TOGETHER, RUNNING QUICKLY OUT OF the tangled vegetation. They stopped when they reached the bridge, and he could just make out their dark shapes, standing back to back as they peered around, looking for him.

He drew in a breath, ready to call again—and they moved

before he could speak, quick as water over rocks. Two of them flipped around beside his hiding place, closing him in. The third swung herself up on to the tree trunk and leaned over, looking down at him.

Her face was hidden in shadow, but she wasn't the girl he had seen before. The dark shape of her head was heavy and solid. Robert felt his throat dry up. Until that moment he had been thinking of any other people around as fellow passengers. Survivors of the same plane crash.

But now—he didn't know. And he was afraid.

The idea of a plane crash didn't fit anymore. So who *were* these people? *What* were they? He didn't know. All he knew was that he had, somehow, become . . . like them.

The woman leaned forward, stretching out her hand. Rough fingers brushed his face, and when he jerked his head away she laughed suddenly. A harsh, mocking bark.

Her head turned slightly, and he heard her sniff the air. When her fingers reached out again, they found the wound on his leg and he yelled, before he could stop himself, at the sudden, sharp pain.

The woman made a quick sound, and the other two bent and took hold of him. They lifted him out of his hiding place like a clump of thistledown, hitching their arms around his back and hoisting him onto his feet. One of them was taller than the other, but they were both male, and strong, and they both smelled the same—an acrid, smoky smell that caught in the back of Robert's throat and made him gag.

They hauled him away from the ravine, dragging him through rough-edged plants that scraped his skin and caught at his fleece. The ground sloped sharply up toward a wall of trees and they pulled him up the slope. The tall one had harsh, rough hands. The short one was gentler, taking his weight when he stumbled.

Toward the top of the slope, they clambered over a huge, gnarled tree root. Between that and the next one, there was a small hole going into the ground. The woman fell onto her knees and crawled into it, feet first.

The other two forced Robert to follow her, thrusting his head into the tunnel. The woman caught hold of his shoulders and dragged him in, edging backward and pulling him after her. Too weak to resist, Robert slid on his side through a tight, earthen tunnel, with soil falling onto his face, clogging his nose and ears. He screwed his eyes up tightly and concentrated on breathing.

After a few seconds, he felt warm air and space around him. He opened his eyes onto a smoky darkness filled with moving shadows. He was lying in some kind of big cave, deep in the earth, and it was crowded with people.

At least, they looked like people. . . .

There were dozens of them, dim shapes, lit by a red glow that came from the far end of the cave. The air was thick with wood smoke, underlaid with something strong and animal, and there was a constant noise of rustling and crackling and whispering.

Little people. Tiny creatures, huddled in a hole in the ground. Little people moving fast and secretly, smeared with the colors of the earth. Faces hidden in the shadows. If he met their eyes, what strangeness would he see there? If he cut them, would they bleed cold sap?

At the far end of the cavern was a vast brazier, punched full of holes. It was four or five times as tall as the shifting figures around it. Its dull light flickered over them, casting distorted shadows onto the rough, earthen walls.

The men heaved Robert up onto his feet again and dragged him down the cave, toward the brazier. The tall man let him go abruptly, but the short one lowered him onto the ground, crouching down beside him. Robert scuttled away until he was up against the wall, with the warm earth touching his back. He huddled there, and his eyes flitted around the cavern, from one face to another.

Out of the blurred darkness and the shifting, indistinguishable shapes came a familiar figure. A girl knelt in front of him, holding out something in one hand. One side of her face was lit red by the brazier, and he saw that it was the girl who had brought him food. He remembered the feel of her narrow wrist, fragile and real in his hand.

She lifted her cupped fingers toward him. He smelled what she was holding and sensed that it was warm. When she put it to his lips, he opened his mouth and let her push it in.

It was a coarse, stiff mash, starchy and full of husks. He swallowed and gagged—and then swallowed again as the next mouthful came at him. And the next. And the one after that.

The girl was scooping the food out of some container on the ground, but Robert was too tired and too weak to look down and see what it was. He just kept swallowing. Once he tried to turn his head away, but the girl slapped at his cheek with her free hand. He opened his mouth again and swallowed the last mouthful, out of sheer shock.

Then he slept.

12

They burned his leg.

The pain woke him without warning, searing into the wound in his thigh. Even before he opened his eyes, he was already tensing his muscles, trying to twist away, but he couldn't move. He was held by dozens of hands, clamped on to every limb. A circle of strange faces closed him in, staring down at him and filling the air he breathed with their smoke smell.

He screamed without choosing to, hardly knowing that the noise was his own, and the pain came again, stabbing at his arm this time. The smoke smell was drowned out by the ugly stink of his own charred flesh, and he fainted.

For days — two? three? — he drifted through a web of whispers and blurred images. People came and went around him, talking fast and low. Muttering in undertones to each other, with their heads close together and their hands moving, sketching meanings that he could not catch.

There was fur underneath him, spread over springy branches that bent with his body. There was fur wrapped around him, tickling his face. He looked out of his cocoon into the hot orange holes of the brazier, which lapped him with its fierce, dry heat.

And all around the voices fluttered and hissed, like the buzzing of flies, like the crackle of burning wood.

Hazily, as his consciousness came and went, he picked at the stream of sound, snatching fragments of sense. He moved his lips to repeat the patterns that came again and again, and, bit by bit, he began to understand.

Lorn . . . Cam . . . Nate . . .

He recognized the names first, learning which head turned at each different call.

Lorn was the girl who had led him there. She sat beside him with food, pushing it at him until he opened his mouth and ate. The sound of her name linked itself to those neat, deft fingers. It wound itself into the strands of her plaited hair and took on the shape of her fine-boned face. Lorn looked after him. And when she wasn't looking after him, she sat in a corner of the cavern weaving threads together to make long, strong ropes.

Cam was taller and stronger. She was the woman who had had him brought into the cave, and she came every day to inspect his wounds. He would wake to find her staring into his face with sharp, steady eyes.

When the fever went down at last, and his wounds began to scab over, it was Cam who moved him out of his cocoon and set him to work by the brazier.

He knew what to do by then, because he had watched the others do it, working in pairs to feed the flames. Whenever he opened his eyes, there were two of them there, toiling away together. Once he recognized the men who had brought him in. The tall one lay on a high ledge, pushing logs into the fire, and every few seconds he called for another one. "Nate!"

That was the short man's name. Nate.

Each time he was called, he pulled a log off the woodpile

and carried it up the earthen ramp to the ledge. It happened over and over and over again. The fire needed to be stoked constantly, almost without a break.

Because they aren't really logs. And small twigs burn through very fast.

When Cam decided it was Robert's turn to help, she sent Nate and the tall man—*Perdew*—to haul him onto his feet. Leaning on their shoulders, Robert staggered down the cavern and crawled onto the ledge. And Cam sent someone else to bring the logs up the ramp.

Bando.

Bando had no trouble lifting logs. He was built like a tree himself, with muscular shoulders and arms like great, twisted branches. He could work all day long without getting tired.

But he had the floating, flitting attention of a moody child. Left to himself he sat on the ground beside the woodpile, playing aimlessly with a little collection of stones. Humming in a deep, hoarse voice, he laid them out and scooped them up, over and over again. The fire painted his heavy face with scarlet, and his shadow loomed bulky and threatening on the wall behind him.

Robert watched the light from the brazier and the shadows on the wall. Every few moments, as they grew duller, he called down to Bando.

"More wood."

To begin with, his call was answered cheerfully. Bando jumped up and heaved a log out of the woodpile, grinning as he waved it in the air. The cheerfulness didn't fade even if Robert shook his head at the log.

"That's much too big."

Bando's grin just broadened as he snapped it carelessly. Like a little twig.

So was it a twig—or wasn't it? What did you call a twig that was as thick as your whole body? Could something be a log when it burned to nothing in a few seconds? How could you talk about the world when all your words were wrong?

But after the first half-dozen times, Bando grew bored. When Robert called again, he didn't jump up. He went on shuffling his stones.

"Bando!" Robert raised his voice. And then—because he was bored, too, and getting tired—he shouted as loudly as he could. "BANDO!"

That was a mistake. Bando was instantly furious. He leaped up and bellowed aggressively, "Do it yourself!"

Then he scooped his stones off the ground and lurched away into a corner.

Robert lay where he was, looking around for someone to come and help him. But all the others were busy, and no one took any notice. Not until the red glow from the fire started to fade. When that happened, Cam appeared below the ledge and yelled up at him.

"What are you doing? Get some more wood on that fire right away!"

"But I can't—" Robert began to protest.

He could have saved his breath. Cam had already moved on to the next job and the fire was still fading. He glared at the brazier, hating it.

There were still a few fragments of label sticking to the can. Soot and scorching had made the words unreadable. *Tomato Soup,* maybe, or *Baked Beans.* Either way, it didn't matter. It wasn't a can anymore. It was a gigantic, glowing monster that needed feeding day and night.

He hated it—but he dared not let it go out. Without being told, he knew that was the worst sin he could commit. He had to get the wood himself.

The ledge was so close to the roof of the cavern that there was no room to stand up, even if he'd been able to manage it. He had to work his way painfully backward, levering himself along to the ramp with his arms and his good leg.

He slid down the ramp to the woodpile at the bottom. It took all his strength to lift even the smallest log and push it back up to the ledge. All the time he was terrified that he would fall and jar his wound. But there was no other way to do it.

And there was no chance to rest. When he reached the top, he could see that the fire was dangerously low. He heaved the log into the brazier and set out again immediately. And all the time, the thick scabs were pulling painfully at his leg and he was sweating in the heat that roared out from the metal walls of the brazier.

By the time he had fetched three logs, he was exhausted, and he was only just succeeding in keeping the fire alight. He lay on the ledge and lowered his head, just for a moment, to catch his breath. He didn't know how he was going to make it down the ramp again.

"Hey!" called a voice from below.

He groaned and opened his eyes, expecting to see Cam glaring up at him, ready to bawl him out for being idle. But it wasn't Cam. It was Nate. He was grinning and holding up a log.

"Hurry up," he said cheerfully. "Or the fire will go out."

Robert hurried. He grabbed the log and pushed it onto the brazier. Immediately another one appeared. Nate held it up to him—and winked.

"Don't worry," he murmured. "I'll fix Bando." He raised his voice. "We work well together, don't we?"

Out of the corner of his eye, Robert saw Bando lift his head. Nate grinned and spoke even louder. "I reckon we make a good team."

Bando came charging out of his corner, with his fists up. "Get out, Nate! You do stoking with Perdew. *I'm* on this team!"

He shouldered Nate out of the way and grabbed the longest log in the pile.

"Here you are!" he bellowed, holding it up.

"That's a bit too big," Robert said cautiously.

Bando grinned and bent down to snap the log. Over his back, Nate met Robert's eyes and winked again. Then he waved a hand and turned away.

Robert waved back gratefully—but he'd gotten the message. Keeping the brazier alight was his responsibility, and staying on the right side of Bando was part of that—unless he wanted to stoke the fire himself. Next time Nate might not be there to help him out.

There were lots of next times. Cam had him stoking every day, for hours at a stretch. It was impossible to think while he was doing it, because he had to watch the fire incessantly. The concentration was exhausting, and the heat was almost unbearable. He knew *Tina* and *Annet* because they were the two who brought him water, in a snail shell, like a great, elaborate urn. They held it between them, lifting it up to the ledge so that he could drink and drink and drink.

Cam seemed to know, by instinct, exactly how much work he could bear. Just as he reached the point of screaming, when he was too exhausted to lift another log, she would appear and call up to him. Her nod meant that he could slide down the ramp and let someone else take over. He crawled straight to his sleeping place and sometimes he fell asleep even before Lorn had brought him food.

The moment he woke, Cam appeared beside him again, sending him back to work with a brisk jerk of her head. She had complete authority in the cavern, and he was too weak to think of disobeying. He worked and slept and worked again in a haze of tiredness.

Whenever he stopped, even for a second, his head exploded with questions.

What happened on the plane?

Was it something to do with the food? The air inside the cabin? The videos?

What was I talking about with Emma?

How can I be so different—and so near home?

There MUST be an answer. . . .

The thoughts were there all the time, boiling in his brain, but he never had a chance to make sense of any of them. He was always too tired to think properly—because Cam never gave him a break in the relentless sequence of work and sleep and work again.

And when he tried to ask her about what had happened to him, she ignored his questions, staring through him as though he hadn't spoken. The others were the same. As soon as he began to talk about his life before the cavern, they fell silent, turning their heads away and wandering off.

It was a long while before he realized that they were doing it to protect him.

AT FIRST HE HAD TO BE SUPPORTED BY TWO PEOPLE WHEREVER he went. The others took turns walking him down the cavern to the brazier, outside to the patch of ground they used as a toilet, and back to the corner where he slept. Those were the only places he saw. Walking between them, even with support, was so painful that it left him sweating and gasping for breath.

To begin with, half an hour's work by the brazier was as much as he could manage. He was almost unconscious by the time they helped him down, and the effort of sliding off the ledge tore at the scabs on his leg. They broke open and healed and broke open again, four or five times. And once the wound on his arm turned red and hot, and they had to put the fire to it again.

At least, this time, he understood that they were saving his life.

As his strength came back, he learned which of them were hunters. *Perdew, Ab, Nate.* He watched them enviously as they crawled into the tunnel, carrying long spears tipped with fragments of tin. He was beginning to long for fresh air and light, and he dreamed about the world beyond the cavern.

But when the hunters came back, they brought strange food that sickened him to look at. Creatures with hard casings and too many legs. Soft, wriggling shapes and slimy things in shells. An animal with thick fur and a long nose.

Beetle. Grub. Snail. Shrew.

He fought against the names that came into his mind, turning his head away and closing his eyes. His dreams of the outside world turned sad and sour, and when the food was served up, he ate it quickly, trying not to know what it was.

HE WATCHED THEM ALL CONSTANTLY, UNDER HIS EYELIDS, trying to figure out what kind of group he was in. He counted twenty-three of them. No small children, no families, no frail, old people. They formed a single unit, and it was impossible to tell how old they were. They all had the same roughened, earth-stained skin. They all moved around the cavern in the same quick, crouching way.

Were they like him? Had they woken up and found the whole world different? He wanted to know but he was afraid to ask, in case they looked back at him with alien, uncomprehending eyes. So he lay in silence, bewildered by the continual shifting movement in the cavern.

Gradually, as the days passed, he began to understand what was going on. The people around him had different skills and different tasks, but they all worked very hard. Food was gathered and prepared every day, some to be eaten immediately and some to be dried and kept. Dew and rain were collected and stored in empty snail shells. Fibers and furs and seed floss were brought in and worked to make all kinds of coverings. And all the time, every day, there was the need to find wood, to feed the insatiable, essential fire.

When Robert could hobble down the cavern on his own, with a stick to lean on, Cam gave him more work to do. One morning she appeared beside him just as he was waking up.

He looked across to the brazier, but she shook her head.

"Not today. It's time you learned something else. You can go and help Lorn."

It was like being promoted out of hell into paradise. Lorn's corner of the cavern was cool and airy, and she sat among heaps of the different fibers she had collected. Settling down beside her, Robert caught the soft, dry smell of them.

"Can you do this?" Lorn said. "Can you braid?"

Robert had a sudden, piercing memory of Emma twitching her hair out of his hands. *That's not braiding—it's tangling!*

"Not really," he said.

Lorn looked up and smiled. "This one is easy. Four strands, going around." She passed over the half-done braid she was holding and picked up some threads to begin another one. "Look."

Robert fumbled for a few moments and then caught the trick of it quite suddenly. His fingers fell into the right rhythm, and Lorn beamed at him.

"You see?" she said. "It's beautiful. Keep doing it until you're sure you're going to remember, and then you can learn another one."

She was halfway through teaching him the eight-strand braid when Cam came past. She didn't speak, but she paused for a second. Looking up, Robert saw her glance at him and then nod toward a dark pile in the corner. Lorn nodded back tranquilly and went on braiding.

"What was that about?" Robert said softly, as soon as Cam had gone.

Lorn smiled again. "You're like Cam. You see everything."

"So what was going on?"

"She was telling me to make you a tunic to go over that fluffy stuff you wear. It'll be twice as warm with leather over the top. Cam must think you're nearly ready to go outside."

Robert reached out and felt a corner of the thin, dark leather. It was what they all wore, made into soft, pliable tunics with a hole for the head and a braided belt. He hadn't realized that Lorn made those as well as the ropes.

Lorn made his tunic—but it was Cam who had given the order. He was beginning to understand that it was how things worked in the cavern. Cam kept track of the whole intricate, busy system of activity, watching the others to see what each one could do. And making sure it was done.

The more he saw, the more Robert understood that Cam was at the center of everything. The others worked hard, but she was the only one who knew the whole pattern. She braided their lives together into a rope that was stronger and more complex than anything Lorn had ever made. Bit by bit he started to grasp how it all came together.

The only one who didn't fit was the man they called Zak.

As far as Robert could tell, Zak had no special job of his own. He was thin and wiry, but he didn't seem to have any particular skills. He helped out with everything. Dess called on him to carry bundles of seedheads. Perdew got him to fill the shells with water. He took orders from Nate and Ab and even Annet. He looked like a general gofer.

And yet—*Zak* was a word full of respect. When he spoke, all the others stopped to listen. And sometimes Cam glanced his way before she gave an order, as if she were checking what he thought. There was a kind of stillness that surrounded him, as though the others were all waiting for him to do something or give some sign.

ROBERT HAD BEEN THERE SIX WEEKS BEFORE ZAK BROUGHT out the drum.

By that time, the feeling of waiting was very strong. Robert still didn't understand it, but he could feel everyone growing tense and quarrelsome. Once he overheard Nate and Perdew murmuring to Zak.

"What's all the delay?" Nate muttered. "Isn't it time for drumming?"

Zak smiled and shook his head slightly.

"It has to be time," Perdew growled. "He's still seeing things double. He needs to make the break—"

Zak put a finger to his lips. Nate looked around and saw Robert watching them. He touched Perdew's arm lightly, and the words died away.

The drum appeared a week after that. Zak brought it out suddenly, with no warning.

It was a small drum, made of thin leather stretched over a wooden frame. One moment it wasn't there, and the next it was lying in Zak's lap. And everyone was staring at it.

They were all in the cavern, sitting in a great ring with the brazier at one end. There had been a lot of food that evening—strips of meat, and grain porridge, and a mash of berries. The brazier was glowing, the woodpile was high, and Ben and Tina had boiled the water and flavored it with some kind of herb. Robert felt drowsy and peaceful.

Sitting in a patch of light beside the brazier, Zak began to drum, stroking the leather drum skin with one hand and rippling his spread fingers over the surface. At first it was a dancing, irregular rhythm, but gradually the beats fell into a steady pattern, slow and insistent.

Then, above the drum beats, came the sound of his humming. His voice hovered and shifted for a second or two. Then it settled on a note that resonated with the pitch of the drum. A long, continuous note.

Cam gave Bando a push. He stood up and lurched across the cave, with his eyes fixed on Zak's drumming fingers. Robert was suddenly wide awake, not knowing what to expect.

There was a heap of leaves in one corner of the cave, piled up like sheets of plywood. Bando stepped out of the circle and squatted down beside them. Sliding his stretched arms under the leaves, he lifted the whole pile, balancing them precariously. The circle parted to let him back in, and he went to where Zak was sitting and laid the leaves down on the ground in front of him.

Zak closed his eyes and waited, still humming softly and running his fingers over the drum.

Bando bent down and picked up one of the leaves. It was like a huge, feathered banner, twice as tall as he was, with toothed leaflets growing in pairs down a central stem. Resting the stalk on the ground, he leaned the leaf gently toward Zak, until one of the leaflets touched his right cheek.

From where he was sitting, Robert could see the front surface of the leaf. The leaflets were bright green, covered with silky hair. Bando lowered the leaf, letting it slide gently over Zak's face. The drumming accelerated abruptly and then slowed again.

"Turn it," Cam said, almost under her breath.

Bando turned the leaf, and it changed dramatically. The underside was a bald, matte gray. For an instant a memory flitted through Robert's mind. He remembered a small plant growing close to the ground, with leaves no longer than his finger. A plant called . . . called . . .

The word slipped out of reach, obliterated by the reality of the leaf in front of him. The leaf that was so tall and heavy that Bando had to brace himself, leaning back to balance the weight as he moved it against Zak's face.

Zak turned toward the leaf, still humming, still with his eyes closed. He touched it with his mouth, opening his lips and running his tongue along the serrated edge of one of the leaflets. Then he put up a hand and clutched at it, crumpling it in his fist and pulling it closer, so that he could sniff at it.

The others were holding their breaths now. Robert could see them all staring, with their eyes wide and their mouths half open. And he stared, too. The leaf dominated the cavern, flinging its tall shadow over Zak's body and onto the earthen wall behind him.

Humming from the back of his throat now, Zak opened his mouth wider, taking in the edge of the leaf. With quick, sharp movements, he bit—and spat. The drumming stopped dead.

And then—at last—he looked. His eyes traveled up the leaf, to the high tip, and down to the base of the stalk where Bando held it against the dusty, earthen floor. He covered every inch of it, and Robert found himself looking, too. They were all looking, following Zak's eyes. Taking in the exact shape of the leaflets and the way they curved away from the main stem. The strength of the stem and the texture of the gray underside of the leaf. The whole physical reality of it.

It's too much, Robert thought. *Too much.* The leaf had become the solidest, most real thing in the cave. But what was he supposed to think about it? Was it good to eat? Useful for making rope? Something that could be dried as bedding?

What *was* it?

He wanted someone to tell him.

That was the moment when Zak named it. He gave a quick, brisk nod. Greeting the leaf and summing it up.

"This is silkskin," he said, in a clear, firm voice.

A long, satisfied sigh ran around the cave. Robert felt everyone relax as the name linked itself to the tall, textured leaf. The sound and the object were twinned forever now. *This is silkskin.*

After a moment, Bando bent over, reaching for the next leaf in the pile. But Cam drew in her breath, just loudly enough to make him look around. Catching his eye, she nodded across at Robert.

Not me, Robert thought, without knowing what the nod meant.

But Bando obeyed Cam, as he always did. Dropping the leaf, he marched straight across the circle. Without hesitating, he bent down and slid his arms around Robert's body, heaving him off the floor.

There was no time to protest. Robert was lifted right off his feet for a second as Bando swung around. Then he was dropped in front of Zak, so suddenly that he crashed to the ground. The fall jarred his wounded leg and twisted it sideways, and the pain made him gasp.

"Be quiet," Zak said. Not unkindly, but with authority.

He reached forward and touched the wounded leg, pulling it into a more comfortable position. Then he looked down at Robert, meeting his eyes.

"Who are you?" he said.

13

"YOU KNOW MY NAME," ROBERT SAID. "I'VE TOLD YOU."

Zak didn't say anything. He just waited. And looked. All around the circle, people were staring at Robert, expecting . . . he didn't know what. He could feel the pressure, but he had no idea what they wanted him to do or say. Wherever he turned, there were eyes glinting in the shadows.

"OK!" he said, when he couldn't stand it any longer. "I'll tell you again. My name's Robert. Robert Doherty."

Zak raised his eyebrows just a fraction. As if Robert had surprised him. "So tell me about yourself, Robert Doherty. What are you like?"

That was an easy question. A school standard. *Write a description of yourself. . . . De quel couleur sont tes yeux? . . . Calculate your own density. . . . Today we're doing self-portraits.* Robert had done it dozens of times.

"Dark brown hair," he said. "Grayish, greenish eyes. My nose is a bit lumpy, but my teeth are good."

Zak's nod was polite, giving nothing away. "And your family? They're the people who know you best. What would they say about you?"

Before he could stop himself, Robert thought of Emma, and his parents, and home. For a second he couldn't speak at all. The torrent of bewildered, angry, terrified questions surged up inside his head. *Where are Mom and Dad and Emma? What happened? How can I—why did I—?*

"What would they say?" Zak repeated, not leaving any space for the questions.

Robert caught his breath and answered quickly, before he was overwhelmed. "They'd say I was a bit of a techie. And good at basketball—because I can reach so high."

The moment the words were out, he knew that he'd walked straight into a trap. A flood of familiar, tormenting images swept up from the bottom of his mind, blotting out everything in front of him.

He was running down the basketball court with great long strides, bouncing the ball in front of him. He saw himself jump for the basket, with his arm held high, stretching, stretching. . . .

Flick.

The picture switched, suddenly and viciously.

Now he was marooned on the edge of a great sea of polished wood, with the gym rising around him, impossibly high and huge. Immediately ahead was the raised white strip that marked the edge of the basketball court. The strip was so wide that it would have taken him three strides to cross it.

But he dared not cross, because of the danger. Beyond that line great feet thundered up and down, ten times his size. If he got caught underneath one of those, he would be squashed flat.

Flick.

Now the picture had changed again. He was sitting in front of his computer at home, chatting in three windows at the same time. His fingers rattled over the keys, making jokes and wisecracking back at his friends, faster than they could reply.

Flick.

He was *on the computer,* all right. But now he was crawling across the keyboard. Every time he wanted to press a key, he had to stand up on it and jump up and down, trying to make his weight register. One letter at a time. i-'-m- -r-o-b-e-r-t- - h-e-l-p--m-e-.

And all the time there was a voice shouting in his head, *Help! Help! Help!* On and on and on. *Help, Dad! Help, Mom! Help!* Anyone would have done that. Even Tosher or Joe. Even *Emma.* But no one was going to help him. No one would come, because he couldn't . . . he wasn't . . .

He wasn't tall or about to play basketball or able to lift his mom off the ground or big enough to arm-wrestle his dad or able to run down the road or draw cartoons or whisper jokes in Tosher's ear (unless he crawled right in) or tease the cat (*How* scary was the cat?) or turn on the television or make a phone call or send an e-mail or get on a bus or buy a candy bar (it would feed everyone in the cavern for a week if he could) or take the remote control away from Emma or play a computer game (What kind of speed do you get jumping from key to key?) or take a bath or clean his teeth or crawl into bed and pull up the covers and pretend that everything was just

the way it

wasn't

anymore.

The whole thing hit him at once, in a split second, a crazy, high-speed collage of pictures that didn't match or make sense. It hit him like a missile, knocking the stuffing out of him. Knocking the *self* out of him. He was swamped by a black wave of loss and despair and never, never, never again. And worse than all that—worse than all the grief and rage and desolation—was a terrible, humiliating shame.

He was no one. Nothing. Nameless.

He was dissolving.

WHEN THE BLACK WAVE DREW BACK, ZAK WAS STILL LOOKING at him. Robert forced himself to meet the stare, expecting— what? Triumph? Sympathy? He didn't know. But he wasn't prepared for what did happen.

Zak closed his eyes. Then he reached out toward Robert's head. His hands found the top of it, tweaking the thick, straight hair. He rubbed it between his fingers and Robert heard the hairs scraping together and felt them pull at the thin skin of his scalp.

Zak's hands ran down his face, over the forehead, around the eye sockets, and across the cheekbones. As they moved on, circling the ears and mapping out the shape of the jaw, Robert felt himself grow solid again. His head. His neck and shoulders and arms. Zak lifted one of his hands and held it up to sniff the scent of the skin. Then he laid his own palm against Robert's, pressing forward. Robert pressed back, feeling his muscles work, measuring his strength.

Zak's eyes were still closed, but his face was sharp with concentration. Robert felt all that fierce attention focused completely on him. Not on *Robert* or *Rob,* but on *himself* as he really was at that moment, crouched in the dark cave. Zak's fingers ran over the leather tunic that Lorn had made and the fleece that Robert had found for himself. They touched the healing wound on his thigh, with a touch as light as thistle-

103

down. Robert remembered the ogre-bird and his fight and the effort and cost of his survival. It stood sharp and clear in his mind, as real as his own skin under the moving hands.

Zak opened his eyes and looked him up and down. All around them the cave was silent, the air as still as standing water. When Zak drew in his breath, the noise resounded like a fanfare.

And Robert knew that he was going to be named.

Zak was going to name him, the way he'd named the leaf. That was why all the others had unfamiliar names. They had all—every one of them—been through the same nightmare as he had. The black water had swept over them, too, and Zak had pulled them out with a name that was real in the cave and the ravine and the dark wood.

And now it was his turn. He was going to take his place in this new life. Then he could forget the lost, high-in-the-air, steel-and-plastic existence of Robert Doherty and be real with the rest of them, down there on the dark ground.

Zak drew in his breath and opened his mouth—

And Robert knew he couldn't take the new name.

He felt the lure of it. He understood the easy, comforting solution—but he couldn't do it. He remembered his own face as he'd last seen it, reflected in the restroom mirror high above the clouds. *That's still me,* he thought. *I'm the same person.* Before Zak could speak, he interrupted, clear and loud.

"My name is Robert Doherty," he said. "I have a mother and father and sister in one of those houses across the park. And I'm going back there, to find them."

He felt the shock of his words resonating around the circle.

Zak didn't move, but Cam darted forward, thrusting her face at him.

"Don't. Be. Stupid," she said. Taking a separate breath for each word. Flinging them into his face like fists. "This. Is. How. It. Is. Accept. It."

Robert was afraid she was going to hit him. He was afraid they were all going to rush him at once, beating him down and trampling on him. But there was nothing else he could do. He had to say it. "I'm still the same person. Even like this. I'm still *me*. And I'm not going to give in. I'm going to find a way of getting back to what I was."

"No!" Lorn said. "That's terrible!"

It was a relief to turn away from Cam. Robert hunted in the shadows on the other side of the circle until he found Lorn's face. She was almost in tears.

"I'm going back," he said gently. Ignoring the others and speaking directly to her. "I know where we are—I saw it from the top of the tree. I'm going home."

A current ran through the cavern, like a ripple in the air. Lorn's eyes widened and Nate leaned forward, as if he were going to speak. But before either of them could make a sound, Bando lumbered forward, looking puzzled and confused.

"You can't go home. You won't be able to get in."

That unblocked the silence for the others. Suddenly they were shouting at Robert, yelling nonsense with a sharp edge to it.

"You're too small to reach the door!"

"Your shirts won't fit!"

"—can't work the computer—"

"—open the fridge—"

"—turn on the TV—"

"—use the phone—"

The cavern was full of ugly, jeering voices. Robert put his hands over his ears, but the others came closer, shuffling on their knees and crowding around him, standing up to spit the words in his ear.

"—can't take a bath—"

"—play with a Game Boy—"

"—eat a Popsicle—"

"—send an e-mail—"

He couldn't keep the sounds out. He couldn't turn off the flood of angry images. They filled the air and beat at his brain, and he braced himself, feeling the anger swell and grow. Waiting for the words to turn into fists, hammering at his body.

Very gently, Zak began tapping at his drum, setting up a rhythm. Gradually the shouts took on the pattern of the drumming.

Ta-ta tap, ta-ta tap.

"You can never go back—"

"—this is all that there is—"

"—all the rest is unreal—"

Ta-ta tap, ta-ta tap.

The drumming kept the same rhythm, but gradually it grew slower and softer. People began to sit down again, sinking onto the floor where they were. The shouts died away, and Robert sensed the pressure lifting. He felt himself becoming less visible, less important.

He subsided, too, finding a place between Lorn and Nate.

Lorn was holding a half-braided cord. It was twisted tightly across her knuckles, digging into the flesh. And when Robert looked up, he saw that she was crying. She lowered her head, avoiding his eyes. He turned away quickly, embarrassed at having upset her.

That brought him face-to-face with Nate. Nate's expression was quite different. As their eyes met, there was a flash of excitement, fleeting but unmistakable. *We need to talk.* Neither of them said it, but it hung in the air between them. Waiting for the right moment.

For now, though, there was silence. Like everyone else, Robert let the drumming take over until the whole cavern was completely quiet and still.

When the last rustle had died away, Zak put the drum down. "Listen," he said.

The red glow lit his face, sharpening its angles. His voice was calm and full of authority.

"Once there was a girl who was lost in a dark wood. . . ."

Perdew and Tina slid surreptitiously back to the brazier as the red glow began to dim. Very quietly, they started lifting the wood again, lowering the logs very gently into the fire, so that they didn't interrupt the story.

14

AT THE END OF THE STORY, THEY SLEPT WHERE THEY LAY, except for Perdew and Tina, who went on stoking the brazier.

And Cam.

Cam went out on her own through the tunnel, into the night. She walked along the edge of the ravine, through the tangle of creepers and thorny vines, knowing that Zak would come.

He called to her softly, from overhead, using her name. Not *Cam*. Her real name. The sound stabbed at her, and she jammed a finger into her mouth, biting it to keep herself silent. Slithering down from the tree, Zak dropped lightly to the ground in front of her. When she tried to turn away, he moved with her, blocking the path. And he said her name again.

This time she lashed out, aiming for his mouth, but he caught her fist and held it high in the air, watching her face.

"I'm not going to cry," she said defiantly.

Zak raised an eyebrow, and she realized that she was already crying. Pulling her hand free, she rubbed it angrily across her eyes.

"He's the one," Zak said.

"He's too new." Cam looked rebellious. "He doesn't know how things operate."

"You know he's the one," Zak said relentlessly.

Cam glanced away, avoiding his eyes. She did know. She

had known for weeks. "What am I supposed to do?" she said.

Zak didn't answer. Not until she looked up and met his eyes. Then he said, "You ought to go with him."

Cam's heart jumped. "How can I go? There's too much work to do. It'll be winter soon." She scrubbed at her face with the back of her hand, getting rid of the rest of the tears. Thinking, *I'm over it now. I can cope. I'm going to make the decision myself.*

If Zak had left her alone for a few minutes, that would have been true. But he went on looking at her. The moonlight caught his eyes and they gleamed suddenly, like a Siamese cat's.

"You have to go," he said. "I'm sorry, Cam, but it's time." He batted her words back gravely. "It'll be winter soon."

Holding his gaze, Cam saw the cold come out to meet her, cruel as a clear January sky. She met his long, blue stare without blinking.

"It has to come from you," he said. "And it has to be him. There's no other way."

And then he was gone, swinging himself up into the dark trees. For a second Cam saw his silhouette moving from branch to branch. Then it dissolved into shadows, leaving her standing, shaken and uncertain, on the ground.

Slowly she walked back to the cavern, struggling to convince herself that he was mistaken. But the battle was already lost. She knew Zak was right.

It was time.

15

Robert woke up the next morning with his own voice echoing in his head. *I'm still the same person. Even like this. I'm still me. And I'm not going to give in. I'm going to find a way of getting back to what I was.*

The words still sounded good. He had reached out and taken a grip on the slippery, impossible substance of his life. What lay ahead was frightening and unpredictable, but he was in control now.

Sitting up, he peered around the cavern, somehow expecting it to look different, altered by the change inside his head. But it was the same as always. Bodies were curled up around the walls, making pools of shadow in the red firelight. There was the usual undertow of whispers and snores and tiny, restless movements. And the same thick smell of smoke.

As soon as he moved, Cam noticed he was awake. She caught his eye and nodded toward the brazier.

"I'm not—" Robert began.

But there was no choice. Cam had already turned away to talk to Annet. Perdew was sliding down from the ledge, and Nate was beckoning Bando over to the woodpile. If Robert didn't take over now, the fire would probably go out.

Angrily, he went over to the brazier and heaved himself up the ramp.

Bando had just woken up, too. He staggered straight to the woodpile, but he was still dazed and sleepy. When Robert called down for a log, Bando pulled at a piece that was jammed in tightly, near the bottom. As he tugged it out, the whole pile collapsed and wood rolled everywhere.

"Why do you have to be so stupid?" Robert snapped. "Why don't you stop acting like a baby and pull yourself together?" He didn't care how loudly Bando bellowed back. He needed an excuse to yell at someone.

But Bando didn't make a sound. He cringed away, like a bullied child, avoiding Robert's eyes and shrinking back against the wall.

Robert felt sick. Revolted. He wanted to slide off the ledge and race out of the cave. To escape from everything. He let himself imagine what it would be like to burst out of the tunnel and run and run, across the short, green grass to the other side of the park.

Lorn dropped her plaiting and came flying across to Bando. Squatting down beside him, she put an arm around his huge shoulders and stretched up to whisper in his ear. Bando shook his head sulkily for a moment or two, but she went on whispering.

Nate was talking to Perdew. He stopped in mid-sentence and came back to the scattered woodpile. Without looking at Bando and Lorn, he picked up a log and brought it up the ramp.

"There you are," he said, squatting down by Robert's feet. "Shove that on to keep the fire going until Bando calms down. Lorn will get him settled in a minute."

Robert glared at the log, not taking it. "Why does everyone keep treating me as though nothing's happened? Didn't you hear what I said last night? I'm *leaving*."

"I know you're leaving," Nate said steadily. "But you're here now. And the fire needs stoking."

"And that's the most important thing in the world?" Robert looked up angrily. "Don't you remember a different life? Without all this endless work?"

Nate met his eyes without wavering. "We don't *remember*. We look forward."

He said it firmly, but his voice was dead. As if he were reciting something. Robert thought of the look they'd exchanged the night before.

"You *do* remember though, don't you?" he said softly. "When I said I was going back—you knew how I felt."

There was no reaction. Nate's face was fixed like a mask.

Robert pushed a bit harder. "You want to go back, too, don't you?" he murmured. "But you're scared."

There was a tense silence. Then Nate nodded at the fire and held out the log again. Robert took it impatiently and rolled over toward the brazier. He thrust the log into the flames, ramming it in so hard that sparks went shooting up to the roof.

When he rolled back, Nate was staring at him. Robert sat up and leaned forward.

"Why don't you come with me?" he said softly.

"I—"

Nate was struggling. Robert understood that he had asked something forbidden, but he knew it was the right question. He said it again, leaning closer so that their heads were almost touching.

"Come with me, Nate. We'll do better if we go together. And you want to come, don't you?"

For a moment, Nate was completely still. Then, very faintly, he nodded. Robert grinned and held out his hand, and Nate took it, gripping it hard. Then he turned and went down the ramp to fetch another log.

Robert closed his eyes and took a long, slow breath. *My friend,* he thought. *He's my friend and he's coming with me.*

When he opened his eyes again, Nate was back, holding out the next log.

"What's your name?" Robert said. Speaking so low that no one else would hear. "What's your *real* name?"

Immediately he knew that he'd made a mistake. Nate flinched and drew back, shaking his head. There was no time to repair the damage. Before Robert could say another word, there was a loud gurgle of laughter from below and Bando shouted up at them, "Get down, Nate! You're in the way. *I'm* doing the woodpile—and I'm racing Lorn. I have to get it straight before she brings the breakfast!"

He came charging over to the logs and began to stack them, lifting them as easily as matchsticks. Nate shook his head at Robert and grinned, holding out the log. "Better take this quickly, before Bando throws me off the ledge."

The moment for questions had gone. Robert took the log, smiling ruefully.

Nate ran off down the ramp, hurrying to catch up with Lorn as she went to fetch the breakfast. Following with his eyes, Robert saw a still figure beyond them, in the shadows. It was Cam. Watching everything.

CAM KEPT ROBERT AND BANDO STOKING NEARLY ALL DAY. LORN brought them water and food, but no one came to take over.

By the evening, Robert was furious and tired and dehydrated.

That was the moment Cam chose to let him talk. As Shang and Lorn began to lay out the food for everyone, she nodded quickly at Dess and Ab, signaling them to take over. Dess came across to the ledge and grinned up at Robert.

"I bet you thought she was going to keep you there all night, too."

"I thought she was going to keep me there for the rest of my life," Robert muttered sourly.

He was so stiff he could hardly climb off the ledge. Letting himself down cautiously, he limped across to the circle that was forming around the food.

He knew, at once, that they were going to discuss what he had said. He could tell by the way people looked at him and murmured to each other. By the way Perdew stopped to examine his wounded arm and leg. By the feeling of tension and suppressed excitement that filled the whole cave.

But he knew, without even thinking about it, that he mustn't start the discussion himself. That wasn't how things were done in the cavern. It was Cam who fixed the times and gave the signals. If he began on his own, unasked, he would break the rhythm of things and lose the argument immediately.

He settled down and took his share of the food in silence, not listening to the muted chatter going on all around him. He was saving all his energy and concentration for a great speech.

Are you really content to live in this hole for the rest of your lives? . . . Don't you want to understand what's happened to you? . . . Don't you want to get back to where you should be . . . to your real size . . . your real selves?

The phrases rang in his mind. As he ate he hunted for

words to trigger people's emotions. Maybe he could persuade some of them to come along on the journey with him.

He was wasting his time. When the moment came, there was no chance to make a speech. Cam waited until the eating had almost stopped. Then, as Bando began to chew at the last roasted grain, she leaned forward, into the firelight.

"Robert," she said. "You've been up the tree with the night bird. You've seen the whole view. Where are we? What are you planning?"

Her voice was sharp. Once Robert would have mistaken that for hostility, but he had been in the cave for long enough to know better now. The sharpness meant she was focused. Whatever he had to say, she would give it her full attention.

Everyone was listening. Zak and Lorn and Perdew. Ab and Dess by the brazier. Nate. They were all waiting for his answer. Even Bando was listening as he sat on the edge of the light, playing with a handful of stones.

Robert closed his eyes and tried to visualize what he'd seen in that long, bleak time in the tree. He knew that *Where are we?* had no simple answer.

"We're sitting in a hedge," he said carefully. Taking his memory of what lay outside the cavern and weaving it together with other, different memories to make a new kind of sense. "This is a hole under the hedge. If you come out of the hole, you're facing into a bit of scrubby woodland. You know that as well as I do."

Cam glanced at Lorn. Leaning forward, Lorn drew one finger along the dry, dusty floor of the cave, making a line.

"This is the long wood," she said. "And the cavern is here, under the wood." She marked a circle halfway along the line, and then used all her fingers to rough up the earth on one side of it. "When we come out of the cavern, through the tunnel, we're looking across at the great trees. But there's a ravine between us and them."

It's not a ravine, Robert thought stubbornly. *It's a ditch.* But he wasn't going to be distracted. He reached over the roughened earth and touched the ground on the other side of Lorn's line.

"If we go the other way," he said, "*through* the hedge, we'll come out onto the grass. In the park." Stretching as far as he could, he drew the shape of the park. Long and roughly rectangular, tapering slightly as it approached the road. "*That's* what I saw from up in the tree. At the end of the park is the road. And across the road is the house where I live. We're not in a jungle. We're not anywhere strange. We're in the place where I've spent my whole life."

"You think you can get there?" Cam said. There was an odd lightness in her voice that was almost like flippancy. "Just because it's familiar?"

"I know it won't be easy," Robert said doggedly. "I'm not a fool. It'll probably take several days to get to the far end of the park, and it's sure to be tough going. But I have to do it. My family must be going crazy, wondering where I am."

He knew he was leaving out the biggest thing of all, but he didn't care. Lifting his head, he looked around the circle, challenging everyone. *What about your families? Are they as near as mine? Don't you want to go home, too?* But no one would meet his eyes, except Nate—and even he stayed silent.

Zak studied the lines Robert and Lorn had scrawled in the dust. He moved his hand over Robert's untidy oblong.

"When you look at this," he murmured, "what do you see?"

Robert didn't reply. It wasn't a real question. Zak let it hang for a few moments and then he answered it himself.

"When I look at it, I see death. It's easy to find a quick death in a big, open space. There's always a gull flying over, looking for something small and tasty."

"At least a gull would save him from having to fight the weasels," Shang said flippantly.

"And the rats." Annet sat back on her heels and preened imaginary whiskers with clawed hands.

Perdew grinned. "Not to mention the stoats—" He wiggled his arm sinuously.

The others began to join in.

"—and the owls—"

"—thrushes—"

"—starlings—"

"—kestrels—"

Bando had forgotten his stones now. He was looking from one face to another, and his eyes were wide and nervous. People were beginning to add gestures to the words, darting their hands into Robert's face, tugging at his hair, flicking his nose with their fingers. Robert tried to brush the hands away, and Zak gave a low, tolerant laugh.

"That's right. Don't pay any attention to them. They're just fearmongering. I can't see you having to worry about stoats and kestrels. You'll have much more urgent problems."

He glanced across the circle, and Nate nodded slowly. "It's very dry out in the grassland," he muttered.

"And there's nothing to eat," murmured Lorn, clutching at her stomach and making a face.

"C-c-cold, too," Tina said, chattering her teeth.

Robert wanted to argue. But before he could speak, Cam leaned forward and rapped him on the mouth.

"Be quiet! You had your chance to tell us about the ground. We listened to your map—now listen to ours. We've only told you about the grassland so far. What comes next, Zak?"

Zak opened his eyes, wide and innocent. "Why don't we ask the one who's been up the tree?" He nodded at Robert. "Go on. Tell us. What's on the other side of the recreation ground?"

"You know perfectly well," Robert said irritably. "It's my house."

Zak's smile was lopsided and scornful, crinkling up one side of his face. Slowly he shook his head. "You're not there yet. After the grassland there's—"

"Another long wood." Lorn drew it in along the far side of Robert's rectangle. "Then the wires. And after those it's the grass where people take their dogs. That stinks."

Tosher's Jack Russell. The spaniel next door. The big red setter from up the road. She was right, of course. Robert had seen them hundreds of times. But no one ever complained—not as long as they stayed on the strip of grass outside the park.

"They're only dogs," he said defensively.

"That's right." Cam smiled benignly. "Dogs are OK, aren't they? Not half as bad as cats."

There was a sudden scuffle in the dust. Bando scrabbled back toward the wall, pulling himself into the shadows.

"Stupid!" muttered Lorn, with a fierce look at Cam. She went after Bando and squatted down beside him, putting an arm around his shoulders.

And Robert laughed. It was involuntary, surprised out of him by the sight of Bando's fear. By the idea of Bando trying to squeeze his great, muscular body into the shadows to avoid an ordinary house cat.

The moment the sound was out, he wanted to call it back, but it was too late. The others drew away from him, sliding out of the light. He was left on his own with Zak, in the center of the cavern.

"Come on." Zak caught hold of his arm and pulled him onto his feet. "Let's take a look at the world outside."

Robert wanted to make the others discuss his plans. He wanted to see if Nate would speak up on his side. But his silly laugh had ruined all that. He let himself be led to the tunnel and crawled through meekly, ahead of Zak.

They came out into the cold darkness. Zak set off immediately, walking briskly over the rough earth under the trees. Robert had forgotten what it was like. He hadn't been more than a few steps outside the cavern, in all the time he was there, and his memory of the tangled, dark wood had faded. He had come to think of it as something like the hedge he'd always known. A little bigger, maybe, but still the familiar mixture of hawthorn and beech and holly.

It was a shock to find himself following Zak over difficult, broken ground, through a great mass of tall, interwoven trees. The little area around the cavern was relatively clear, worn smooth by constant comings and goings. But once they were beyond that, nothing was level. They were traveling over heavy clods and boulders, with cracks opening up between them. Every step was a separate effort.

The darkness was full of whistling, pulsing noises. Zak

moved through it easily, looking backward and forward and all around, as though he could see things that were invisible to Robert. Robert struggled after him, tripping and stumbling.

They walked through the trees for ten or fifteen minutes. Then Zak turned right sharply, and they came out into an area of tall, slender plants. Their stalks were no thicker than Robert's leg, but they rose high into the air, twenty or thirty times as tall as he was. Way above him, in the moonlight, great, seeded heads drooped heavily.

Long grass in an angle of the hedge. Where the mower misses it.

Robert remembered hunting for lost tennis balls in patches of grass like that. Stooping and parting the stems to look down at the damp earth. Now the grass towered over him, and the ground under his feet was thick with creeping stems snaking under and over each other.

Zak stepped through the jointed stalks, careful not to catch his feet. Robert followed, clutching at them to save himself from falling.

There's only a small patch of long grass. Just a few steps. Once we're out into the short grass there won't be any problem.

But it took them well over half an hour to get to the shorter grass. By that time Robert was cold and tired, and his leg was aching. He thought longingly of his two fur blankets, back in the warm cavern, but he kept moving, following Zak as he pushed his way between the pale stalks.

As they neared the end of them, Robert felt the air grow fresher, stirring around him. Zak looked back and beckoned, and Robert stepped forward eagerly, longing to stride out at last. Expecting open space and short, cropped grass.

The reality was quite different. He came out of the high

grass into a field of stiff, shoulder-high leaves, like growing corn. But corn would at least have left the ground bare between individual plants. Here there was no bare ground. No distinction between separate plants. The stiff leaves rose out of a mat of tangled roots, denser than anything they'd come through so far.

Robert was determined not to be beaten. He could see Zak looking at him, watching for some sign of dismay, but he didn't waver. Stumbling past Zak, he peered over the cropped tops of the grass blades, looking down toward the end of the park. Toward his house. It was still a long way off, but he was hoping to see the lights on the first floor. Surely they should be visible above the hedge at the far end of the park?

There was nothing. Only darkness.

It took him a moment or two to realize that the ground in front of him was sloping upward. It was only a very slight slope, too shallow for him to have noticed when he—in the old days. But now it was enough to block out everything beyond.

He turned around quickly, to say something casual before Zak could guess his disappointment. But Zak had disappeared.

He was standing all alone in the dark, open grassland.

His first reaction was anger—and then a stubborn determination to carry on with what he had been doing. He began to battle his way forward over the roots, toiling up the slope to reach a place where he might get a better view.

But he had taken only twenty or thirty steps when a wave of fear swept over him. Away to his left, the grass rustled suddenly and he spun around, terrified. *It can't be anything seri-*

ous. I'm only in the park. But that was as unreal as a fairy tale. The reality was being alone, in the dark, in country where he couldn't move fast or see far. And all around him—circling in the sky, hidden in the grass—were hungry predators with eyes that could see in the dark. He began to run—

And immediately Zak was there, gripping him by the arm and spinning him around.

"You want to get lost?" he said lightly. "There's nothing in that direction. Only grass and more grass."

"Why did you leave me then?" Robert was so angry that he could hardly speak.

"You've got to know what it's like." Zak let go of his arm and took a step back. "You have to be prepared if you're really determined to go on that journey."

"Of course I'm still going!" Robert snapped. "I told you."

He began to struggle the other way, thinking he was heading back toward the long grass. But after a few seconds Zak called to him from way over on the left.

"It's better here!"

Robert turned, feeling foolish and furious. He could hear Zak whistling softly, to guide him in the right direction—and he imagined a smug smile accompanying the whistle. He clenched his fists, longing to strike out at something. *Why is he so sure he's right?*

But there was no smug smile. When Robert found him, Zak was standing at the edge of the long grass, in a patch of clear moonlight, and his face was grave and slightly sad.

"Well?" he said gently.

All Robert's anger drained away. "It's frightening out there," he said.

Zak nodded approvingly. "That's the first lesson to learn. Fear's not an enemy. It's essential for survival. We're nice little mouthfuls of protein and fat, and wherever we go there'll be hungry eyes watching out for creatures like us."

Robert made a face. "I'd rather be at the top of the food chain."

Zak grinned ruefully. "You think you'll get back there by trekking across the park?"

"I have to find my family. I need to know what's happened to them. And they might—"

"Be able to help?" Zak said mockingly. "Is that what you're thinking?"

"No!" Robert said. Too fast to be convincing.

Zak laughed softly in the darkness. "Give it up. There's nothing they can do. Small is an alien planet, and that's where you live now. Why don't you change your mind and stay?"

Suddenly it seemed shockingly easy to say yes. Easy and safe. It took all the determination Robert had to meet Zak's eyes and give the difficult answer. But he made himself do it.

"I'm going back. I've decided."

Zak gave him a long, steady look and then shrugged and set off back to the cavern. There was no smile. No sign of agreement.

But Robert had a sudden, odd sense of having gotten it right.

III

The Journey

16

THE NEXT MORNING, WHILE EVERYONE WAS STILL IN THE cavern, Robert stood up and announced what he meant to do. He wanted them all to understand that he hadn't changed his mind.

"I'm going to find my family." He pitched his voice loudly enough to carry to the farthest corners and looked straight down the cavern toward Nate. "Anyone who wants to come along is welcome, but I'm not waiting around for company. I'm going to start collecting food today. As soon as I've gotten enough, I'll begin the journey."

There was an immediate rush of whispering. Some people turned away, and others looked uneasily at Robert.

Lorn was appalled. Robert saw her face change as he spoke, and when he finished she came straight across the cavern to argue with him.

"You're crazy. You'll die. Remember what it was like before—when you were by yourself? You'd have died then, if I hadn't helped you."

"So help me again," Robert said. "Come with me."

Lorn shuddered and went away.

But she didn't give up. When he went out to begin his hunt for food, she scrambled down the tunnel after him. As he set off through the trees, she followed him, pulling at his arm and trying to drag him back.

"You haven't got a clue what you're doing! There are beaks

out there . . . and boots . . . and soccer balls. Everywhere you go there'll be something dangerous. And you'll be too small to defend yourself. Don't you understand? We're *weak*."

She bent down and grabbed at the biggest stone she could hold, straining to heave it out of the ground. When it was free, she pushed it down the slope, putting all her energy into the effort.

The stone slithered slowly for a few feet and then stopped, lodging against the first plant it met.

"You see?" Lorn said bitterly. "I can't even throw it hard enough to bend a piece of *grass*."

Robert stood and waited. The stone was balanced precariously. After a few seconds, it slipped around the grass stalk and began to slide down the slope again, gathering momentum as it went. When it reached the foot of the slope, it skittered over the edge of the ravine and went on falling, tumbling through the plants to the very bottom. There was a faint splash as it hit the water in the bottom of the ravine.

"I don't need to bend the grass," Robert said. "All I need to do is set out. It may take a long time, but I'll get there in the end."

"No you won't. You'll get *eaten*." Lorn looked wretched. "Why won't you listen? We know what it's like, out there in the grassland."

Robert had spent the whole night thinking about that. "I'm not going across the grassland. I'm going to stay in the trees, all along the edge of the park. It'll take a bit longer, but it ought to be safe."

"*Safe?*" Lorn was trembling now. "You think you can be safe somewhere else? The cavern is the only good place."

"It's just a hole in the ground," Robert said. "Wouldn't you rather be home?"

But Lorn was too upset to go on talking. When he tried to explain, she put her hands over her ears and went off, leaving him on his own.

PERDEW WAITED UNTIL LATER ON TO HAVE HIS SAY.

His chance came in the afternoon, when Robert and Bando were stoking the brazier. Bando was restless and unhappy, turning his head away and sulking whenever Robert spoke to him. Suddenly Perdew appeared beside the woodpile.

"I'll do that," he said.

Bando muttered gruffly and lumbered away, and Perdew stepped into his place. He didn't speak immediately. He went up and down the ramp half a dozen times, moving the wood with brisk efficiency.

When there was plenty of fuel on the fire, he took a step back from the woodpile and stared up at Robert. "I don't get it," he said. "What's the point of this journey of yours? You think something's going to happen? Just because you trek across the park?"

"I want to see my family." Robert pushed at a log that was sticking over the side of the brazier. "Why does everyone think that's weird?" He looked down sharply. "Don't you want to go back and see yours?"

Perdew's expression went blank, shutting him out. "That's another life. Things are like this now, and that's how they're going to stay. You'd better get used to it."

The fire flared briefly, sending their shadows shooting up the opposite wall. "You think *this* is a life?" Robert said.

Perdew turned his head away. "It beats starving to death."

"Oh, come *on!*" Robert said impatiently. "Think what your life was like before you were small. The food. The houses. And television and music and all the machines to make things easy. And just not having to *work* all the time. Don't you *remember?*"

Perdew glared, his face twisting as though Robert had said something obscene. "You want to learn the hard way, don't you?" he muttered.

He walked off abruptly, nodding at Bando to tell him to take over the woodpile again. Watching him go, Robert saw Nate in the shadows, gazing at him. *What about you?* he thought. *Are you different from the others? Or will you try to persuade me to stay here, too?*

When Cam finally signaled that he could come down, Nate was waiting at the bottom of the ramp.

"I've got to cut up some fruit," he said. "For drying into strips. You can give me a hand if you like."

Robert was longing to crawl into his corner and lie down, but he followed Nate across to the fruit supply. All week Tina and Annet had been bringing in big, crimson fruits like the one Lorn had left outside his burrow when he was on his own. There were dozens of them stacked against the far wall of the cavern.

Nate picked up a couple of blades from beside the stack. "These knives are pretty clumsy," he said. "But they're OK for cutting the fruit off the stone."

They were hardly knives. Just pieces of metal broken off a can and beaten thin. Robert picked one up and weighed it in his hands.

"Show me what I have to do," he said.

Nate chose one of the fruits and rolled it into a space. With a knife in his hand, he began to move around the fruit, scoring it from top to bottom, to mark it into neat sections. He was on the far side, half hidden, when he spoke suddenly, not looking at Robert.

"I'll come."

"What?" For a moment, Robert was too startled to take it in.

"I'll come with you. To the other side of the grassland." Nate's hand moved, cutting another section. "If you still want me to."

"I—" Robert had to catch his breath before he could speak. The relief of it took him by surprise. "You're certain?"

"We'll go together," Nate said.

He crouched down suddenly and scratched with his knife on the ground. Robert thought it was part of the job they were doing, and he walked around the fruit to get a better view. Nate scratched again. His hand was shaking slightly as he made the marks.

S-T-E-V-E-N

Still not understanding, Robert crouched down, beginning to read the word out loud. "St—"

"No." Nate shook his head quickly. "Don't say it." His voice was tense and unhappy.

Robert realized what he was looking at. "Your real name," he said softly.

Nate bent over, scrubbing the letters out with the palm of his hand. Then he looked up and grinned. "Better get this fruit finished. So we can start collecting supplies for the journey."

THEY DIDN'T MAKE ANY KIND OF FUSS ABOUT IT. BUT THEY began to spend two or three hours outside every day, gathering extra food. Hardly anyone else realized that the two of them were working together.

But Cam noticed.

Robert was aware of her all the time, watching them from the shadows. She never spoke to him, or to Nate, except to give them work to do, but Robert felt her eyes on them, taking in everything they did.

She knew just how much (how *little*) food they had managed to stockpile so far. She noticed the state of his leg as he limped around the cavern. She listened when he and Nate talked about their route. Every time she looked at him, Robert expected her to ask when they were leaving.

But she never said a word.

IT WAS THE RAIN THAT BROUGHT EVERYTHING TO A HEAD. IT came down out of a cold gray sky, driving hard and steady into the trees. Even from inside the cavern, they could hear it battering at the leaves outside. On and on and on, hour after hour.

Usually, rain was welcome. While it was falling, they hid underground, to avoid being drenched and overwhelmed by the heavy raindrops. But the moment it was over, Cam sent everyone scurrying outside. Robert had seen it happen two or three times when he was too weak to join in. The water shells were scoured out and filled to the brim, and the cavern hummed with activity.

But that day was different. There was a strong wind driving the rain straight at the mouth of the cave. Dess went out early and got caught in it, and he came back soaked and shaken. Rainwater trickled down the tunnel and made muddy pools on the floor of the cavern. Cam snapped at Annet because she stepped in one and slid into the blanket pile.

The whole cave was steamy and close, full of impatient people with nothing to do.

After a while, they started to look at Zak, but he pretended to ignore them. He squatted by the nut supply, bent over his drum, with his back to the others. He turned the drum in his hands, beating soft snatches of rhythm that broke off halfway through, unresolved.

The stopping and starting increased the restlessness. Petty arguments began to simmer. Annet shouted at Bando for stirring up the fire. Lorn complained about the smell of Dess's drying tunic. Perdew and Tina began a stupid argument about coiling ropes. There was no peace anywhere.

All at once, Zak rippled his fingers hard across the drum skin, swiveling around as he sat, so that he was facing into the cavern. There was a sudden hush, and people began to sink down, settling into a circle. Waiting for the story to begin.

But there was no story. Instead, in the silence, Zak held out the drum to Cam.

"Now," he said.

Cam took the drum and held it on her lap as she began to speak.

"The frost is almost here. If there's a journey to be made, it has to start immediately. Or not at all." She turned to look at Robert, and everyone in the cavern turned with her. "Are you ready to go?" she said.

"Yes, I am." Robert said it defiantly. It was the only possible answer. "I'm leaving as soon as it stops raining."

"*We're* leaving," Nate said, from the other side of the circle.

Almost everyone was taken by surprise. Robert saw the shock of it, going around the circle. Only Cam didn't look startled.

"You're both going?" she said. One of her eyebrows went up mockingly. "That miserable heap of food you've scraped together is meant for *two* of you?" She slapped her hand against the drum skin, making a flat, ugly sound. "Don't be stupid. You need a lot more than that. You need nut meal and fruit strips and roasted grain. And you need more than two people."

"We do?" Robert let his eyes travel around the cave, fixing on one face after another. Lorn and Perdew and Dess. Tina. Annet. Bando. On and on around the circle, while people shifted awkwardly, looking away. At last his eyes came back to Cam. "So who else is coming then?" he said sarcastically.

Cam didn't hesitate. She met his gaze full on.

"Zak's coming."

This time the shock was audible. Everyone gasped together, and even Robert felt it. *Zak can't go. What will we do if he's not here?* No one said the words out loud, but he could hear people muttering them. Nate glanced across at him, looking stunned.

Cam sat calmly, waiting for the protests to die down. Then she said, "If you're set on going, we might as well do it properly and learn what we can. You need a strong group to go with you." Her voice was firm and practical, not leaving any room for argument or discussion. "Nate will do fine, but you need Zak, too. To make sense of what you find out. And one more person. To coordinate the group."

I can do that, Robert thought.

But Cam didn't give him a chance to speak. She looked briskly around at everyone else and then she said, "I'm coming, too."

There was a terrible, shocked silence.

17

ROBERT EXPECTED THE SILENCE TO END IN AN ARGUMENT. He'd forgotten that nobody argued with Cam. They were used to doing what she said, and they did it now—looking sulky and scared but obeying her orders.

She didn't attempt to explain her reasons for going. She just started on the work.

"Robert and Nate—go and choose our batpacks. We'll need the biggest ones. With strong straps. And we'll need to do something about water, too. Tina can look into that. And Ab."

Annet was sent to the food supply, to take out enough to fill four batpacks. Bando went after her, to help carry the food, and Shang was dispatched to sort out the warmest furs. While everyone was scurrying around, Cam took Lorn and Perdew aside and talked to them for a long time.

Before everyone went to sleep, the supplies had been gathered together and everything was arranged.

It rained again in the night, but by dawn the sky was clear. Robert and Nate crawled out of the cavern together and stood watching the preparations. In the gray half-light, Annet laid out the four batpacks on a dry patch of ground in front of the tunnel entrance. The others stood around while she and Shang doled out enough food to fill the packs, making neat piles on the pieces of leather.

There were strips of fruit and handfuls of nut meal. One or two squares of dried meat—tough and nourishing to chew.

Some cracked, roasted grain. There was far more than Robert and Nate could ever have collected on their own, but when Robert looked down at the heaps he thought how pitifully small they seemed.

Lorn and Bando came out of the tunnel, bringing three small shells, stoppered with twists of leather. Lorn had made rope nets for the shells so that they could be tied on top of the batpacks.

"They'll see you through for a day or so," she said. "If there's a night without dewfall."

Nate went to help her. The shells were already full, and they were heavy and awkward, but they didn't hold a great deal of water. It was impossible to carry much. Cam was gambling on being able to collect dew as they went.

The whole journey was a gamble. They would have to forage for extra food and find a new shelter each night. And, somehow, they would have to keep warm while they slept, even though they had no way to make a fire. The temperature was dropping all the time and, if the weather was bad, they might even be facing frost.

Cam knelt down to make up her pack. She rolled the leather square neatly, tucking in the ends so that nothing leaked out. Then she wrapped the whole thing in a blanket with the fur turned inside.

"We need to get going," she said.

Zak was already knotting the plaited strings around his bundle. He looked sideways at Robert. "Strip your mind," he muttered. "Forget what you think you know. Whatever you're imagining, this will be different."

Robert mumbled some kind of agreement and reached for

one of his own pack strings. But he hadn't made the roll well enough. As he tightened the string, one end fell open, spilling nut meal on the ground. Lorn shook her head at him and squatted down to demonstrate. As her small, deft hands made up the pack, she leaned sideways to whisper to him.

"Why are you doing this? Why don't you want to stay here in the cavern with the rest of us?"

Zak turned around sharply. "Let him alone, Lorn. It's decided. And he needs all the confidence you can give him." He frowned down at Robert's pack. "Better if he ties that himself. He needs to know how."

"I do know how," Robert said.

He took over from Lorn, tying the first set of strings around the roll she had made. Nate held the bundle against his back while he slipped the second set of strings over his shoulders, bringing them back under his arms, and knotted all four ends together on his chest.

When the whole thing was secure, Bando brought the shell of water, and Nate lashed it tightly on to the top of the bundle, settling it firmly into position and checking all the knots.

"That's fine," he said. "All you've got to do now is carry it." He made a face, adjusting the strings of his own pack.

Cam and Zak were waiting to leave. Each of them was holding a long stick with a sharp piece of tin spliced into the top. Nate and Perdew had made them, grinding down the edges of the tin with hard, heavy stones and lashing the blades into place with plaited cords. The weapons looked awkward and top-heavy.

"These won't cut skin or bone," Perdew said, holding a

spear out to Robert. "If you need to attack—go for the eyes."

"And remember that birds notice movement," said Nate. "But mammals can smell you."

Robert took the spear, trying to picture a battle in which he might use it. But it was clumsy and unwieldy, and his mind would produce only grotesque cartoon images.

"Think small," Zak said softly. "We won't survive without weapons."

Robert nodded, only half-believing him.

All four of them were ready now, but they loitered for a moment, waiting for some kind of farewell. Robert could see the others hesitating, too. Wanting to wish them good luck. Not wanting to make too much of all the dangers.

It was Bando who broke the silence. He walked up to Zak, holding his hand out solemnly.

"Have a good time," he said. As though they were going on vacation.

Gravely, Zak shook his hand.

Bando moved on to Cam and then to Nate and Robert. "Enjoy yourselves. Hope the weather's good. Don't do anything I wouldn't do."

Cam's mouth twisted, but she didn't say anything. She shook Bando's hand and then turned away down the slope. Zak fell into step behind her.

Robert hesitated for a second. He caught Lorn's eye and struggled for something to say, some better kind of good-bye. She was the one who had saved his life, and he wanted her to know that he realized it. He wanted to say—

But there was no time to find the words. Nate was walking

off as well now, expecting him to follow. He couldn't afford to lag behind. All he could do was smile at Lorn and hold her eyes for a second longer.

"See you soon," he muttered.

She bent her head. "Soon, I hope," she said.

Then he was off after the others, feeling the weight on his shoulders and using his spear like a staff.

When Robert caught up, Nate stopped to let him pass.

"Best if I go last," Nate said.

Robert nodded, knowing he was being protected. Glad not to be left at the back. It was reassuring to hear Nate's soft, light footsteps close behind him.

They climbed down to the bottom of the slope and turned left, along the edge of the ravine. It was too dark to see the ground under their bare feet, and they had to feel it carefully, before each step, picking their way between tall plants and knee-high boulders. It was awkward at first, but gradually they settled into a steady rhythm, walking in silence and following Cam's lead.

As the sun rose, her shadowy shape in front of Robert turned from gray to earth-brown, with the batpack dark against her shoulders. She walked with a long, relaxed stride, looking left and right as she went. Robert could see her sniffing the air and tilting her head to listen to the rustles all around them and the clarinet calls of the morning birds.

Zak walked quite differently, staring down at the ground and frowning, as if he were thinking through a problem. Robert wondered how long he had spent in the woods, living on wild food and hiding from rats and owls. His face was thin and weathered, but it was impossible to tell how old he was.

How long could someone last, living that life?

The question jarred uncomfortably. Robert pushed it away and tried to stop thinking. He began to copy Cam, listening and looking and sniffing as he walked, using all his senses to pick up what was going on around them.

The sounds and the smells changed constantly. Leaves creaked over his head, grains of earth moved beside him, and the air carried strange, shifting scents that dispersed before he could recognize them. The forest was full of small signs and messages, but most of them were beyond his understanding. When Cam stopped for a moment, or stepped around something on the ground, he had no idea what she had noticed.

At midday they stopped to rest and eat. Robert was exhausted. He lay flat out on the ground, with his leg throbbing and his arm aching. It was a long time before he could bring himself to sit up and unwrap his pack.

The others didn't say anything about his weakness. But he could see Cam watching him as they ate. When she had finished and remade her pack, she lay down and put the bundle under her head.

"Time to sleep," she said briskly. "I'm going to have a couple of hours before we go on. You take first watch, Nate."

Robert wanted to say, *You don't have to do this. I can cope.* But Cam had already closed her eyes, and Zak was settling himself to sleep as well. Nate stood up, grinning down at Robert.

"Take the chance while you can. Cam won't give us much rest once we get beyond the long wood."

Robert shrugged and stretched out on the ground again—just for a few moments, just to humor Nate—and fell asleep instantly.

Toward the end of the afternoon, they began to approach the edge of the long wood. The ground grew rougher under their feet, lying in loose, unstable clods, and the air moved more freely, striking cold against their skin. Robert began to notice patches of bright, fierce color littered among the trees—red and lurid green and a bright, raucous yellow.

"Perdew's treasure trove," Zak murmured sarcastically from behind. "He would fill the cavern with bits of polyethylene and cellophane—if we let him."

Robert could think of hundreds of uses for something waterproof and easy to cut. "Why not?" he said. "What's the problem?"

"Can't you see how they catch the light? How they draw your eye?" Zak sounded impatient. "That stuff is no good for us."

Robert would have argued, but Cam called suddenly from in front of them.

"Beak!"

There was no mistaking the urgency in her voice. She and Zak threw themselves forward onto the ground, and Nate caught at Robert's arm, dragging him down.

"What—?" Robert's spear tangled itself with his ankle, and he fell with a bump.

"Keep still!" hissed Nate. "Keep absolutely still! And shut your eyes."

They were lying flattened between two boulders, breathing into the damp earth. From just in front, Robert heard sounds of movement. A quick, jerky rustling. Two or three seconds of silence. Then another rustle.

Keeping his eyes closed was unbearable. He felt exposed and helpless, unable to defend himself. Without raising his head, he opened one eye, just enough to see through his eyelashes.

He saw crumbs of earth hanging together in clods. And, beyond the clods, the top of Cam's head, with the water shell tipped forward on her shoulders. The water had soaked into the leather stopper, and it was dripping, very slowly, onto her hair.

Suddenly a huge, speckled head appeared, looming over the shell. Its eye glared horribly, unblinking. Its beak was as long as Cam's whole body. With irregular, mechanical movements, the beak tapped at the tilted water shell, trying to dislodge it.

Lorn's ropes held out. The shell barely shifted. And Cam herself was as still as a stone, even when the beak brushed her cheek, coming away from the shell. She stayed rock steady as the cruel beak lifted.

Then the bird pounced.

It stabbed suddenly downward, aiming close to Cam's head, and Robert drew in his breath sharply, unable to keep silent.

"Stay still!" hissed Nate, so softly that the sound hardly carried as far as Robert's ear.

The great bird pecked down, once and twice and three times. Then it straightened abruptly, dragging up and backward. Out of the ground came a long, grotesque serpent with a body five or six times as long as Cam's. Its pink flesh was mottled and ridged, and it stretched elastically as the cruel beak pulled at it. It gave out a smell like nothing Robert had ever come upon before—fleshy and close and raw.

The bird jerked it free of the ground, dropped it, pecked twice, and picked it up again. Then it hopped away toward the light, with the serpent writhing in agonized contortions in midair.

Robert's whole body was shaking. He had pushed the memory of the ogre-bird to the back of his mind. Now it was surging up again. He could see the yellow, inhuman eye coming down at him and feel the savage beak ripping at his flesh.

Nate put a hand against his back. "Are you all right?"

Robert nodded, taking great gulps of the cold, fresh air.

"That's only the beginning," said Zak, getting to his feet. "There'll be worse things than that before we're done."

"I know there will," said Robert.

"Not tempted to change your mind?"

Robert shook his head and scrambled up, staggering slightly as he straightened his pack. Zak gave him a small, grave smile, and set out after Cam, who had already started walking again.

THEY EMERGED FROM THE LONG WOOD JUST AFTER SUNSET, when the horizon was still streaked with red, away to the right. The trees ended suddenly, and the travelers stepped out onto a patch of bare earth. The air around them was cold, and above them the sky spread wide and open.

Ahead, waist-high grass stood in stiff blades, cropped square at the top. The ground rose slightly, so that they couldn't see more than a few minutes' walk into the grass, but somewhere farther ahead a long, dark shape loomed up, black against the fading sky.

There was just enough light to see that it was a wall of trees, very thick and high. Much denser than the long wood they were leaving. Robert had the impression of an artificial shape, squared off like a building. The trees were tangled together so closely that they formed a single, gigantic block. In the dim light, it was solid and forbidding.

"That's what we're heading for," Cam said. "We should be safe in there."

Robert shuddered, imagining the darkness under those black trees. But there was no alternative. The tree wall blocked the way ahead of them, stretching off to the left into the distance.

Nate narrowed his eyes, studying it. "Good place to spend the night."

Zak nodded. "But we ought to wait for the light to fade before we cross the grassland."

They crouched at the end of the long wood, watching the bright sky. Gradually the colors around them drained away, and the shapes blurred until the tree wall was barely visible. They could just make out the mass of it, rising out of the grass ahead.

"One at a time," Cam said softly. "Aim for the nearest bit."

She went immediately, as soon as she had finished speaking, crouching low to run through the stiff grass. For a moment Robert could see her hunched back, with the stick held high in her hand. Then she melted into the darkness.

"You go next," Zak said.

Robert bent and moved forward into the grass. The darkness was deceptive. Cam had disappeared very quickly, and he assumed he would catch up with her in a few seconds. But he ran until he was out of breath, and the tree wall seemed no nearer. His spear kept getting tangled in the grass stems, and the grass blades tore at his tunic and scraped his arms until he had to slow to a careful jog. He could hear Nate and Zak behind him, moving easily, but he resisted the temptation to look over his shoulder. All his attention was focused on the ground ahead.

By the time he reached the end of the grassland, he was exhausted. And he still hadn't reached the tree wall. He was standing on the edge of a strip of rough, black ground as hard as stone. Beyond that strip the wall reared up, filling the sky.

He crouched in the grass, glancing left and right and over-head. But it was too dark to be certain of anything. He could hardly see the ground in front of his feet, and the night played tricks on his eyes, forming and re-forming mysterious, insubstantial shapes.

In the end, he stood up and ran recklessly, stumbling on the rough, hard ground. Three times he tripped and fell, skinning his hands and knees on the rocky surface, but he was up again instantly, racing for safety.

As he came close to the tree wall, he realized that the thick network of branches didn't reach right down to the ground. The trees began to branch just level with his eyes. Looking up, he could see a continuous curtain of needled branches, dark and heavy as wrought iron. Looking down, he saw the trunks rising straight and massive out of bare earth like a line of ancient pillars.

The trees had a strong, resinous, aromatic smell. It drifted toward him as he ran. When he reached the wall at last, he ducked his head and went in under the branches. Inside, there was space to stand up straight, and the scent of the trees was almost overpowering.

"Hey," said Cam's voice softly, from above.

He looked up into thick shadow. Inside the wall itself, the branches were bare of needles. They ran in all directions, forming an intricate scaffolding that went up and up, as far as he could see.

"Here," Cam said.

Robert's eyes began to adjust to the darkness. Now he could see the crouching mass of her body, lodged in an angle between two branches.

"How do I get up there?" he called.

"Walk along until you get to a trunk. That's the easiest way. Then you can climb up—and go anywhere you like."

Ten steps took him to the nearest trunk. It was far too big to grip, but the bark was rough enough to give plenty of footholds. Robert tucked his spear through the strings of his pack and climbed the trunk as if it were a rock face. When he reached the first branches, he began to work his way toward Cam. The thick, bitter smell of the trees filled his nostrils.

By the time he reached the place where Cam was perched, the others were already there. Zak was settling back against the trunk, and Nate was straddling a branch, whistling as he unwrapped his pack.

"We'll eat now," Cam said.

It was a bleak meal, with no fire and nothing to drink. Each of them sat on a different branch and they ate in silence, listening to the noises of the night. There were a hundred questions Robert wanted to ask, but he was too tired to put the words together and the others seemed remote and detached.

As soon as Cam finished eating, she rolled up her pack and settled herself on the branch, pulling her fur blanket around her. "I'll sleep now and watch later. Wake me at dewfall, Zak. Robert can have the third watch."

Turning her back on them, she wedged herself firmly into the place where she was sitting. A moment later, they heard her breathing grow slower and deeper.

"You heard the orders," murmured Nate. "Don't waste good sleeping time."

Robert unrolled his bat fur and fidgeted around in the branches, trying to find a place that felt secure. It wasn't easy to relax like Cam. The branch was hard, and he was afraid of falling. It was a long time before he went to sleep.

18

THE CAVERN WAS FULL OF ANGER. AND BELOW THE ANGER WAS a slow, cold fear that seeped into every action and every sentence.

Lorn felt it as soon as she opened her eyes in the morning. If she went out, she could taste it in the air as soon as she crawled back through the tunnel. She saw it in people's eyes, when they sat eating or separated to work.

No one spoke the words, but she knew what they were thinking. *Cam's gone. Zak's gone. They've abandoned us. Who's going to figure out what needs to be done? Who's going to tell us how things are?*

On the fourth day without Cam and Zak, it all came to a head.

Lorn had taken Bando out collecting wood. By the time they had hauled it all back to the cavern entrance, it was almost too dark to see. Lorn kept watch anxiously while Bando snapped the logs into manageable lengths. It was a relief when the wood was short enough to push through the tunnel.

Bando went ahead, dragging it, and Lorn scrambled after him. When they emerged into the cavern, they found Perdew cooking grain. He had an old can lid balanced on the edge of the fire, and the air was full of the rich scent of roasting seeds.

"Smells good," Lorn said.

Perdew didn't react. A week earlier he would have looked around and smiled.

Lorn was left on her own to carry the logs across the cavern and stack them on the woodpile. Bando shuffled off, working his way around the lair. The others were sitting singly, waiting to eat. No one spoke to Bando, and he began to fiddle with the blankets, pulling at the fur and twisting the corners.

I ought to find him another job, Lorn thought. She could see that people were getting annoyed. Annet snatched the blankets away, and Dess pushed at Bando with his shoulder. *He needs some more work to keep him busy.*

She tried to think of something, but she had been looking after Bando all day and she was too tired to invent anything else.

It's all falling to pieces.

At least when the food was ready, everyone came into a circle to eat. There was a drizzle of conversation about practical things, and Ab even made one of his lugubrious jokes. But everyone laughed too long, as though they were desperate to fill the silence.

Bando was still restless and uneasy. He chomped at the grain, chewing noisily and spitting the empty husks fiercely at the side of the brazier. They clung there, sizzling and scorching.

"Stop it!" Lorn said. "What's the matter?"

Bando looked sullen, turning his head away. His heavy jaws moved laboriously, still chewing.

"You know what's the matter," Perdew said impatiently. "He's wondering. Aren't you? Aren't we all? He's thinking, *How far have they gotten? What are they doing now?*"

"We won't find that out for a long time," Lorn said. She reached for another seed and cracked the husk under her foot, picking it off and flicking the bits over the top of the brazier.

"They shouldn't have left us," Bando said peevishly. "Why did they have to go? How long till they get back?"

He was looking at Lorn. Suddenly they were all looking at Lorn. And Bando's question was rattling in the air.

Lorn felt a surge of panic. She knew—surely they all knew?—that Bando's question was unanswerable. There was nothing she could say. She knew they needed a reply, but she had nothing to give them. *I can't—*

And then the power came.

Without thinking consciously, without figuring it out, she knew what she had to do. She stood up, walked across the circle to the woodpile, and pulled out a long, straight piece of wood. Then she began to walk toward the tunnel, pulling the wood behind her. The cavern was totally silent.

She walked slowly, dragging the wood over the ground so that its tip marked out a deep, straight groove. Gradually the others turned, following her with their eyes. When she reached the tunnel opening, she stopped and looked back along the line she had made. It stretched right down the side of the cavern, from the brazier to the entrance.

"They're going a long way," she said at last. "It'll take weeks. But even long journeys finish in the end, if you keep walking."

"How *many* weeks?" Bando said insistently.

They all knew it was a stupid question.

But it was the question everybody wanted answered.

Lorn could see them all waiting for her to speak. Perdew and Dess. Tina and Annet. Ab and Minnow and Shang . . . so many faces, all wanting the kind of simple answer that she would have to give Bando.

I can't—

But already her mind was moving, calm as a machine, visualizing the journey. She guessed at the distance and the time—and then doubled her guess. When she spoke, there was no hesitation.

"I think it'll take them about three weeks to get there. Maybe four. And the same to come back."

She felt the tension loosen as people sat back and relaxed. They should have known that the numbers were sheer guesswork. But speaking them out loud had given them a kind of authority.

"Seven weeks overall then," muttered Dess.

"More like eight," Ab said carefully.

They all started discussing the figures, the cautious ones—like Ab—allowing extra time and the optimists thinking of reasons to reduce it.

Bando was the only one who didn't join in. He squatted down beside the line that Lorn had made, shuffling backward along it. When he reached the tunnel entrance, he pulled out the branches that closed it off and went outside. Lorn heard him scrabbling around overhead.

"What are you doing?" she called. "It's dangerous out there."

The scrabbling went on for another moment or two. When Bando crawled back in, he re-blocked the tunnel awkwardly, with one hand. His other fist was clenched tightly.

"What have you got there?" said Dess.

Bando didn't answer. He hurried across to Lorn's line and squatted down again, spitting into his fist and rubbing both hands together.

Lorn went over to see what he was doing, and he opened his hands to show her what he had. He was holding four pebbles. One gray, one black, one brick red, and one a dull yellow ochre.

"Zak," he said. "And Nate and Cam and Robert."

"That's nice," said Lorn, not really understanding.

She would have waited until he explained, but she suddenly saw, out of the corner of her eye, that the fire was burning very low. Shang was supposed to be looking after it, but he was arguing with Dess. Lorn hurried down the cavern to remind him.

When the fire had been rescued, she turned around and discovered that Bando was crouched right behind her. He was placing his stones very carefully onto the journey line, one beside the other, a couple of steps from the beginning.

When the four stones were in position, he stood up and studied what he had done. Then he bent down and rearranged them, so that the red stone was in front.

"Cam leads the way," he said.

"That's good," said Perdew's voice, from behind Lorn. "That's very good, Bando. We'll move the stones a little further each day. Then we'll know how they're doing."

No we won't, Lorn thought. *That's silly. We won't know anything.*

She spun around and saw that Perdew wasn't alone. Half a dozen of the others were with him, carrying handfuls of leaves and little sticks. Stepping around Lorn, they began to lay the leaves and sticks along the outside of the journey line, so that it was marked off and protected from careless trampling.

That's silly, Lorn thought again.

But they didn't look silly. They looked solemn and intent. Watching them, Lorn understood that they weren't just being ridiculous. What they were doing was a serious game. Like the games Zak made them play.

19

Under the dark trees, it was very still. Opening his eyes the next morning, Robert felt the air around him, heavy and scented. The network of bare branches inside the tree wall was separated from everything else by the dense layer of heavy needles on the outer surface of the wall.

Lying curled among the branches, he was suspended in a cool, hushed space. Glimpses of light and movement came from beyond the needles, but he felt completely detached from them. From one side of the tree wall to the other, it was no more than a minute's walk, but straight ahead the trees stretched away out of sight.

Nate reached out from farther along the same branch and nudged him, nodding sideways. "Look at the spiders."

Huge webs spanned every space in the outside surface of the wall, stretching from one dark green, needled branch to another. Seen from inside the wall, they were striking and dramatic, silhouetted against the pale sky and hung with dewdrops. The speckled spiders waited in their hiding places, ready to pounce, invisible from outside, but horribly plain from where Robert and Nate were lying.

Birds' legs strutted past, and once or twice a sharp beak stabbed into the leaf wall near Robert. But he wasn't afraid. Not even when a huge, wet nose snuffled along the edge of the path. All those things were beyond the trees. The thick needle leaves concealed him completely, and their strong smell masked any other scents. Inside the wall he was in a secret world.

For two days they traveled uneventfully through that world. The earth under their feet was dry and dusty, and nothing grew in it except the tree trunks themselves. They were able to walk steadily, without too much scrambling, and the days fell into a comfortable rhythm of traveling and rest.

On either side of them, beyond the walls, they saw the light change through the day. They could tell when the sun was shining brightly, but under the trees the shadows hardly altered. It was always dark and still. There was no noise except the tramp of their feet and sometimes the soft sound of Nate whistling under his breath.

Even when it rained outside, it was dry under the trees, and the thick outer walls muffled the noises beyond them. Robert began to feel that the only real things in the world were their own footsteps and the rise and fall of their breathing.

They walked in the early morning and again in the evening, until it was too dark to see the tree trunks in front of them. At night and in the middle of the day, they climbed into the branches and rested. Robert was still too weak to walk for more than two or three hours at a stretch, and whenever they stopped he fell asleep immediately.

It was on the third day that he saw the runners. It was just after sunrise and he had woken up first. He walked to the edge of the trees, to peer at the sky before they set out. The air was full of a fine, drizzly mist, hanging low on the ground, and everything beyond the tree wall was blurred and indistinct. He couldn't see even as far as the edge of the grassland.

In the old days, he would never have been out so early. If he had woken at all, he would have pulled up the covers and reckoned on another fifteen minutes in bed. But he was beginning to like the fresh dawn air and the way the sky changed as the sun came up. Standing just inside the shadow of the trees, he took a long breath and gazed out at the hazy light seeping through the mist.

And then the ground began to shake underneath him.

It was faint at first. For an instant he thought it was just an odd tingling in the soles of his feet. But it grew stronger, second by second, until he knew that it was not his body but the earth that was trembling.

Earthquake, said his brain. But that was wrong. What he could feel wasn't a sudden, catastrophic jarring. It was a steady beat.

Bam. Bam. Bam.

Not a sound, but a vibration. It caught him off balance, and he staggered slightly.

"Take care," Zak called softly from behind. "Keep still."

The drumming grew stronger, as though the ground was getting ready to explode. It was impossible to distinguish between sound and vibration now. He sensed them both together, with his whole body. But he had no idea what was producing them. Falling onto his hands and knees, he inched forward until his head was just beyond the edge of the trees, peering out into the mist.

It blanked out everything except the small space in front of him. For a moment he couldn't see anything.

157

Then they were there in front of him, thudding onto the path, huge and impossible. He knew what they were. He recognized the patterns, even magnified a hundredfold. *Nike. Adidas.* They thundered down through the mist, one after another—three times, four times, five times as tall as he was—with their strips of silver glinting. They came out of nowhere, beating against the ground and then disappearing upward, too close to make any sense. He could smell the strong, sour sweat soaked into them, and see the puff of dust as their soles hit the ground.

Rolling onto his side, he looked up, trying to see more than feet. Vast shapes rose up into the mist—up and up and up. It was like staring at skyscrapers. The air swirled around them, stirred up by their movements. He felt the chill of it against his face. He felt the ground shake as they passed.

He felt everything shake.

Until that moment, he had hardly thought about the end of the journey. He was simply bolting home, like a little child, taking his troubles to be solved. At the back of everything, he was thinking, *They'll fix it. They'll know what to do. All I have to do is speak to them.*

But how do you speak to a skyscraper?

My mother, the apartment building. My father, the office tower.

He had known—but he hadn't understood. Not at all. Not anything.

He lay there watching the monstrous figures vanish into the mist. There were five of them altogether. Even after they had gone, the air was still moving. It still smelled like sweat.

After a long time, Nate came and squatted down beside him, laying a hand against his back.

"You should have warned me," Robert said when he was sure he could keep his voice steady. "I didn't realize how *big* people are."

The hand on his back went very still for a moment.

"Don't be stupid," Cam said harshly, from behind Nate. "*We're* people."

Robert rolled over, facing into the shadows, and the others stared back at him. Cam and Zak and Nate. Small. Earth brown. Dressed in bat leather and plant floss.

People.

The word flapped around them emptily, huge as a marquee. His mind flicked back and forth, trying to make it fit them all. The three in front of him. The runners. His mother and father and Emma. Himself.

People. All people.

He couldn't do it.

What's the point of words, if they don't fit the way things are?

It was Cam who made him go on. She walked over and jabbed at him with the blunt end of her stick.

"If you stay there, a beak will get you. Get back under the trees. Start walking."

"What's the point?" Robert said dully. "Even if we manage to get there, we won't be able to do anything."

"I thought you wanted to find out who made you like this," murmured Zak. "To understand."

"What's the use of understanding if you can't *do* anything? I just didn't get it. I didn't realize how small we are. We can't do it on our own—"

"Don't!" Nate said sharply, interrupting him. Cam and Zak began to chant, in angry, sarcastic voices.

"Size
Makes you wise!
And growing
Equals knowing!
But shrinking
Stops you thinking,
And once you're small
You're no use at all!"

They went on chanting it until Robert pulled himself off the ground and started walking. He snatched up his stick and went ahead angrily, without waiting for them. There seemed to be no purpose in it, no purpose in anything, but he walked forward anyway. He kept to the middle of the trees, as far away as possible from the light on either side. Staying in the shadows, where there was nothing to see except the trees rising up and up above him, in an unending network of bare branches.

20

THERE WAS NO MIDDAY REST THAT DAY. ROBERT KEPT WALKING obsessively, pushing himself harder and harder. Not leaving room to think. He strode out in front, concentrating on the next clod and the next stone and the incessant struggle to keep moving. When his leg began to tremble, he stopped and sat down to take food out of his pack, but he ate on the move, chewing with the same mindless determination that drove his feet.

He could hear the others behind him, but he didn't look around or wait for them to catch up. He didn't want to talk to any of them, not even Nate. As long as he kept walking, on his own, he could forget what he was—what they all were. He could forget the questions that boiled below the surface of his brain.

What are we doing?

What's the point?

He refused to let them take shape, making sure that his mind was completely occupied with practical matters about what to do with his feet and how to get around obstacles. Those were the only realities. Everything else was abstract and unnecessary.

BY LATE AFTERNOON HE HAD WON THE BATTLE. WHEN HE stopped to gather his strength, his mind rested, too. He was several minutes ahead of the others, and he sat under the trees on his own, chewing a handful of nut meal and gazing idly into the distance.

He was almost ready to start again before his brain connected with what he was seeing. It took shape gradually, in front of his eyes. While he walked he had been aware of very little except the ground under his feet and a shadowy darkness ahead, stretching on and on, apparently without end.

Now he realized that the darkness had taken on a different quality. Ten or fifteen minutes' walk away, he could see the last of the trunks that marched down the center of the tree wall. A little way beyond that, the open space was closed off by a curtain of heavy, dark needles, overlapping each other in great, sculpted curves. They were almost at the end of the wall.

But at the end, rising up through the thickness of the outer surface, he could see a tall, looming shape. It was pale and solid, like a great, stone tower. Behind it, between the needles, he glimpsed the red and gold of the setting sun.

He rolled his pack, tied the strings hastily, and pulled it on, grabbing his spear and hauling himself to his feet. Without waiting for the others, he hurried forward, curious and impatient.

The thing he had seen was brutally man-made. The massive sides sloped slightly inward toward a top that was level with the summit of the tree wall. The surface was rough and grainy, set with huge boulders larger than Robert's head. He scrambled around it, running his hands over the boulders and peering up between their shadows.

There were no windows or doors. It was not a tower. (*How could it be? Who would build a tower small enough for him to walk around?*) It was a solid pillar, made of concrete. The far side was set with huge rusty rings, placed one above another, too high for Robert to reach. Anchored in the rings—contorted around them in ugly, twisted knots—were five long metal cables, each one as thick as Robert's body. They ran ahead horizontally, drawing parallel lines through the air. Impossible lines that went on and on without sagging or breaking.

With his head flung back, Robert stared up at them, imagining how smooth and easy they would feel under his feet. It would be easy enough to climb the pillar. He could plant his feet on the projecting boulders, dig his fingers into the grainy surface of the concrete, and pull himself up into the sky. Up and up and up, until he reached the highest ring. Then it would be simple to scramble over the ring and out onto the broad, taut surface of the cable. And he would be able to see.

He had actually put one foot up on a boulder when Cam came charging at him. She seized his shoulder and dragged him backward.

"Don't think of it! Don't even *dream* of it! Are you crazy?"

"Leave me alone!" Robert said fiercely. "I'm tired of scrabbling around in the mud. We'll be ten times as quick walking along the metal."

"Ten times as dead! Do you want to set yourself up for every bird in the whole park?"

"She's right," Nate said, coming up behind her. "You know she's right. And what if you fell?"

Robert didn't want to listen, but he knew they were talking sense. He dragged his eyes away from the straight, easy path through the air and forced himself to look along the ground, at the alternative.

Beyond the concrete pillar, there was a narrow stretch of open grassland. And slicing through it, running straight across in front of them, was a deep gorge. To the right, it went under the cables, disappearing into thick scrub, but in the grassland it was plain to see.

The cables ran over the gorge and into a patch of giant trees that stood separately, rising up and up into the sky, so high that their tops were invisible. Their trunks were like castles, and their branches ribbed the sky.

Real trees. Oak and beech and maple.

They needed to follow the cables into the great wood, but there was no way to get there without crossing the gorge. Robert walked forward to the edge and peered down.

The sides were so steep that they were nearly vertical. Plants grew thickly all the way down, almost hiding the small river that trickled slowly along the bottom. Some of the plants were brown and dry, but there were plenty of green leaves. Robert could see several clumps of grass spikes, heavy with grain.

Zak and Nate came up behind him, one on each side.

"That's not an easy climb," muttered Nate.

Zak looked down into the gorge, measuring it with his eyes. "It'll be even harder to get up the other side."

Robert looked from one to the other, wondering whether they had any better ideas. But if they had, there was no chance to explain them. Cam came past the concrete pillar, peered down into the gorge, and nodded approvingly.

"That's great," she said. "See all that grain down there? Just what we need. I bet there are snails, too. Maybe even some fish. We'll be able to stock up on food before we go on."

"We need to be careful," Nate murmured. "You can't be sure—"

But Cam didn't listen. Without giving Nate a chance to finish, she sat down on the rim of the gorge and started to lower herself into it. Within a couple of seconds, she had disappeared. All they could hear was an occasional scraping sound as she slithered over bare stones.

"Looks like we're going down there," Nate said.

Zak shrugged. "She hasn't left us any choice, has she? We can't afford to get separated. Come on."

He turned around and knelt down, letting himself carefully over the edge. Nate grinned at Robert. "You next."

Robert knelt down to look into the gorge. "Do you really think it's safe? There could be anything down there."

"That's right." Nate sounded amused. "Scary, isn't it? Want to run away instead?"

Robert made a face at him and started to climb down, clinging tightly to the plant stems and stopping every few steps to disentangle his spear. As soon as he was below the rim of the gorge, Nate came after him, climbing quietly and neatly.

They were about halfway down when they saw Cam and Zak. They were on a ledge, almost at the bottom of the gorge, and Cam was kneeling beside a boulder, jabbing at something with the sharp, metal tip of her stick.

"See!" she hissed when she saw them. "I told you!"

Robert and Nate scrambled down to join in. Half hidden behind the boulder, clinging to its underside, were three great, coiled shells. It was still light enough to see their dappled, spiraling patterns. Cam slapped the side of the largest one exultantly.

"This kind is good to eat. Help me get it off the stone."

It took all four of them to roll the shell. It was stuck hard to the base of the boulder and, even with their arms spread wide, they couldn't get a grip on its smooth, rounded sides.

In the end, they broke it off with a combination of running and leverage. Cam pushed the tip of her stick under one edge of the shell, and the other three ran past her, flinging their whole weight against the side of it. It made a loud, juicy sound as it came away, flopping onto the ground with a squelch.

The soft body quivered back into the opening, but Cam was already jabbing at it with her stick, twisting it so that the metal tip caught in the creature's flesh.

"Don't just stand there!" she snapped. "Hold on to the shell so I can pull!"

The creature was contracting as fast as it could. Cam held on tightly, digging her feet into the earth, but the shell just slithered toward her, drawing her stick into its opening.

Zak and Robert threw themselves down on top of it, anchoring it to the ground. Nate went to help Cam as she leaned backward, tugging hard on her stick. For a moment they were deadlocked. Nothing moved.

"Pull!" Cam said.

Zak and Robert hooked their fingers over the rim of the shell and pulled backward. Nate clamped his fingers around the spear, just below Cam's. All four of them heaved as hard as they could, and slowly the pale, fleshy body was dragged out of the shell. It came free suddenly, with a revolting wet, sucking noise, and Robert retched and turned his face away.

That was what saved their lives.

As Robert turned, he caught a movement down in the leaves below them at the bottom of the gorge. For a second his brain struggled, making no sense of what his eyes were telling him. The thing was too big to see. It took up too much of the dim, shadowy space. It couldn't be—

Then it moved again, and his mind kicked into action.

A long, furry monster was snaking along the bank of the stream, under the cover of the leaves. Its body was tense and sinewy, flattened against the ground. Its head alone was as big as he was, with round ears set close against the skull and eyes that gleamed black and sharp.

It met Robert's eyes and moved again, inching closer. With horrible clarity, he realized that he was within its range, that it was poised, ready to spring forward when he turned to run away. He felt himself tense with terror. The creature moved forward again and the cold black eyes flicked over him, alien and indifferent. . . .

And suddenly his terror was swept aside by a flood of rage. This thing (what was it—stoat or weasel?), this *thing* thought he was a helpless victim. This *thing*—

There was no time to plan, no time to shout to the others. He moved instinctively, fired by fury. Snatching up his spear, he threw himself forward, not away from that ugly head, but toward it. His mouth opened instinctively in a huge, formless yell and he lifted the spear high above his head.

"YAAARRRHH!!!"

The monster was startled. Its head jerked up, and it drew back, hissing. Robert ran on, without thinking, without reckoning the risk, putting all his weight behind the sharp tip of the spear.

His reach was pathetically, pitifully short, but he was moving fast and his aim was good. As the monster recovered, it came down at him, with its mouth wide open. Warm breath swamped him with a stench of rotten meat, and sharp, yellow teeth glinted all around him. Bracing himself for the pain of those teeth, he jabbed into the gaping, fanged hole, aiming as far back as he could.

In that instant he didn't care about getting hurt. He didn't care if he *died*. All his energy, all his anger, were concentrated into one savage blow.

Just as the jaws started to close, the metal point of his spear connected with the soft palate, and he threw himself right into the monster's mouth, ramming the spear home. Twisting it as hard as he could. The creature wrenched its head away, rearing up and pulling the spear out of his hands. Hissing horribly, it shook its head from side to side, trying to dislodge the point.

Without the spear Robert felt utterly helpless. His anger drained away and he would have bolted—but Nate came running past him, dodging around to one side of the huge swinging head. Grabbing handfuls of reddish brown fur, Nate began to haul himself up, gripping the shaft of his spear with his teeth.

The monster tossed its head harder, but it couldn't get rid of him. Straddling its neck, Nate took hold of his spear with both hands and pushed it hard into one of the small, round ears.

The creature shrieked and jerked its head sideways, knocking him to the ground. Robert's weapon came flying out of its mouth, clattering toward his feet, but Nate's was in too deep to loosen. It shook its head again furiously, and Robert scrambled to snatch up his spear. Lifting it high, he ran at the monster again, yelling with all the breath he had.

"YYAAAARRRHHH!!!"

Simultaneously Zak shouted from the other side, racing in with his spear aimed at the creature's underbelly. Cam charged forward with hers, screaming and stabbing the air. And Nate jumped up and joined in the yelling, waving his arms ferociously.

For one second the monster glared at them all, hissing and baring its teeth, with Nate's spear waggling grotesquely in its ear.

Then it turned and ran, still shaking its head to try to get rid of the burning pain. They all slithered down after it, waving their arms in the air and yelling triumphantly, until they had chased it into the shadowy clumps along the side of the river.

Then—shouting and exultant—they scrambled back up to the ledge and heaved at the fleshy creature they had pulled out of the shell. Working together, they hauled it up the side of the gorge, heading back into the tree wall.

They sat under the dark branches and ate the meat raw, leaning back against one of the tree trunks. Cam used the tip of her spear to slit the body open and dig out the guts. Then she and Nate hacked the meat into pieces and doled it out. It was cold and wet and salty, but they sucked the juices and chewed the pallid flesh until their jaws ached.

As they ate, they talked and laughed and grinned at each other, telling and retelling the story of their fight.

"The way you went for that monster—it was the bravest thing I've ever seen!" Cam said. She leaned forward and clapped Robert on the back.

"I didn't really—"

He was going to say something modest, but before the words were out he knew they were wrong. This wasn't a time for modesty. The others laughed at him, shaking their heads and pushing more meat into his hands.

"Don't deny it," Zak said. "You're brave. And you're pretty strong, too."

"As strong as a horse!" Cam said. She flexed her muscles dramatically.

"As strong as a bull!" Nate jumped up, pulling Robert with him. Robert clenched his fists and threw them into the air.

"*Yes!*" He began to strut around dramatically, half mocking and half serious.

"As strong as an elephant!" Cam shouted.

She bent and lifted two of the batpacks, one in each hand. Robert looped the strings over his shoulders and laughed at her.

"I can carry more than that!"

Zak and Nate brought the other two bundles and Robert laughed again, bending to take the extra weight. Cam gave him a push to set him walking, and he began to march around the tree with all four bundles on his back. The others drummed on the trunk with their hands, chanting in turn.

"You're as brave as a lion!"

"As strong as a giant!"

"Bones like iron!"

"Muscles like steel!"

"You fought the monster!"

"You made it run!"

They were drunk with triumph. Robert marched around and around, stamping his feet and waving his fists above his head. He could feel the power in his body and the fierce strength of his will. Whatever was ahead, he could cope. He had faced a nightmare creature ten times as big as he was— and he had beaten it.

"We drove it away!" he shouted. "I fought it, Nate fought it, we all fought it—and it ran away from us. We beat the monster!"

Zak's hands thundered against the tree trunk. "We beat the monster—and Cam found food. More than we can eat! She found the shell, and we pulled it off the rock!"

Robert laughed aloud. "You're brilliant, Cam! You know where to look for food! You know what we can eat! You're the leader!"

They were all waving their arms now, shouting into the darkness. Zak started to sing a loud, wordless tune, like a fanfare of trumpets, and they took up the rhythm, marching around the tree and slapping their hands against the trunk. Their triumph surrounded them like a wall of fire, and they marched on and on, until Robert began to stagger under the weight he was carrying.

Then they climbed up into the dark trees, scrambling up and up, until they were higher than they had ever been before. Until they couldn't see anything, in any direction—up, down, or sideways—except the maze of spreading branches.

Wedging themselves together in the crook of a single branch, they slept instantly, sated and exhausted.

21

In the night, Robert was sick. He leaned over the edge of the branch and vomited, not stopping when his stomach was empty, but retching on and on, uncontrollably. His whole body was in revolt.

Zak and Nate held on to him, keeping him from falling, but he was hardly aware of that. Not until the spasms died away and he flopped back against them.

"Are you ill?" Cam said sharply.

Ill was bad. He could hear it in her voice. Automatically, he shook his head, without any idea whether he was right.

"Let him sleep," said Zak.

Nate pulled Robert into the center of the branch and wrapped him firmly in two bat furs. Fleetingly, Robert recognized that the second one was Nate's own blanket, and he wondered how Nate would manage without it. Then the thought disappeared, because he was asleep.

The next time he woke, it was almost dawn, and Nate was shaking his shoulder.

"You have to wake up now. We need to get across the gorge before it's light."

Robert lifted his head, blinking and trying to pull his wits together. Nate leaned closer, studying his face.

"Are you feeling better?" He sounded anxious.

Robert sat up, wriggling his shoulders and turning his

head. He felt weak and drained, and curiously detached. But not ill.

"I'm fine," he said.

"Good. Let's roll up the blankets and get going then."

Robert peered along the branch. "Where are the others?"

"In the gorge." Nate pointed down through the trees. "They've been there for hours, ever since you went back to sleep. Didn't you realize?"

Robert shook his head.

Nate grinned. "Cam said we couldn't leave here until we'd collected some grain. She wasn't too pleased when I said I was staying up here, to keep an eye on you."

Collecting grain meant heaving at the stiff, jointed grass stalks until they keeled over. Then, when the seed heads were within reach, the separate grains had to be stripped out of their sockets. The grains were big and unwieldy, and it was exhausting work. Robert wasn't surprised that Cam had wanted Nate down in the gorge.

"You should have woken me up," he said. "I ought to be helping, too."

"Didn't want you throwing up all over the food." Nate grinned again. "Come on. I'll take the blankets."

He pulled them free and rolled them up quickly, tucking both of them under his left arm. Then he ran along the branch and began to climb down, one-handed.

Robert followed more slowly. As soon as he started to move, he realized how weak and stiff he was. Climbing down made his whole body ache. By the time he reached the bottom of the tree, he felt like sitting still for half an hour.

"What's wrong with me?" he said crossly. "I wasn't this feeble yesterday."

"You're doing OK," Nate said. "That fight will have drained all your energy—and you're still recovering from the night-bird attack. Don't push yourself too hard."

Robert made a face. "I'm not the one doing the pushing."

"Don't let it bother you," Nate said. "It's part of Cam's job to nag us. And she may be nagging a bit harder because—"

He broke off, as though he'd changed his mind, and turned to go. But Robert caught his arm, holding him back.

"Why would she be nagging harder? What do you mean?"

Nate was obviously reluctant to say any more. But Robert tugged at his arm impatiently, and after a moment he went on.

"It's just a feeling I've got. Cam's really tense. And it's odd that she and Zak have *both* come on this expedition. I've been wondering if . . . there's something going on. Something bigger than they've told us."

"It's not *their* expedition," Robert said. "It's ours. And Cam's always tense, isn't she?"

Nate hesitated. "Maybe she is. Since you came, anyway." He shrugged. "I've probably been imagining things."

He gave Robert a quick tap on the arm—a light, friendly pat—and set off abruptly toward the gorge.

Robert forced himself to follow. It was hard work trudging through the grass. When he reached the gorge, he sat down and rested for a few seconds before he let himself over the edge. He was intending to climb down, like Nate, but his arms ached so much that he took the easy option and slithered most of the way to the bottom.

Cam and Zak were waiting by the stream, with the bat-packs at their feet. The packs were bulging with grain, and two of them were already wrapped in fur blankets, with water shells and spears lashed into place. The other two packs were waiting, with the single remaining spear lying loose on top and the shells ready beside them.

As Robert straightened up at the bottom of the slope, Zak gave him a sharp, searching look.

"Will you be able to manage your pack?"

"He'll have to," Cam said briskly. "We can't hang around here. It's already too light to be safe. We should have been up the other side and into cover a couple of hours ago."

Nate picked up Robert's pack, weighing it in his hands and frowning. Robert reached out and took it from him.

"Stop worrying. I thought I was as strong as an elephant."

He swung the pack into place on his back. It was even heavier than he had expected, and he staggered slightly, taken by surprise. Immediately he was aware of Cam's eyes on him.

"I'm fine," he said quickly. "I was just settling it on my back."

Cam didn't look convinced. But all she said was, "You don't want it on your back just yet. We'll have to carry them on our heads while we cross the stream. Hurry up and fix the rest of your gear. We need to start."

"Don't fret," Nate said. "You and Zak can start if you like. I'll help Robert with his pack."

Cam nodded grudgingly, and she and Zak let themselves down into the water. They began to splash across, taking slow, noisy strides.

Nate lifted the pack off Robert's back and laid it on the

ground again, rolling it in the bat fur and heaving the water shell into position on top. He lashed the whole bundle together securely and tucked the last spear through the strings.

Robert looked apprehensively at the water, wondering how long it would take him to cross with all that weight on his head. He imagined himself lagging behind Nate, with Cam yelling at him from the far side.

Nate glanced up and caught his expression. "Why don't you start now?" he said gently. "No need to wait for me. It'll only take me a minute to fix my gear, and then I'll be right behind you."

Gratefully Robert picked up his pack. With the water shell in place, it was almost more than he could lift, but he was determined not to give in. He sat down on the bank of the stream and swung the whole load onto his head, steadying it with one hand. Then he slid down into the water.

It was very cold and almost waist-deep. To take a step, he had to fight the pressure of it, steadying himself against the flow. Once he was away from the bank, it took all his strength to stay on his feet. He shuffled across, a step at a time, inching his way through the numbing cold.

He was about halfway across when he heard a noise from behind. It was a rustle, hardly loud enough to reach him, but there was something about it that made him stop.

Before he could turn to look back, the rustle was drowned out by a loud, desperate shout curdling into a scream. Robert whipped around then—almost falling over—and saw a sight that froze his heart.

There, on the bank he had just left, was the long, furry

monster they'd driven away the day before. It was unmistakable. He could see its round head and its black eyes and the thick, clotted blood in its ear, from the wound that Nate's spear had made. And in its mouth—

No! said his mind. *No, it can't—*

It was a fixed, terrible image. Unthinkable and real. The malevolent, narrowed eyes. The lifted head, heavy and brutal. The clamped, murderous jaws.

And hanging from the jaws, hanging slack now and stained with blood—

"Nate!" Robert shouted. *"Nate!"*

"Don't look!" Zak's voice said sharply, from behind him.

At the same moment, in a frenzy of splashing water, Cam came charging past, screaming at the top of her voice, with a spear lifted high in her hand.

Robert started to struggle after her, but he managed to take only a couple of steps. Before he could cover any distance, the monster on the bank lifted its head and looked hard at Cam. Then it turned and slipped off into the bushes, still with Nate's body in its mouth. And Cam was on her way back, shouting at him now.

"Get to the other side! Before it comes after us!"

"But . . . Nate—"

"Don't be a fool," Cam said bitterly. "It's too late for that. Come *on!*"

She grabbed Robert's arm and dragged him with her, pulling so fiercely that he almost lost his footing. Zak was kneeling on the opposite bank, waiting to help them out of the water. All three of them were soaked and shivering, but Cam didn't let them stop for an instant.

"Get up the bank," she snapped. "Don't look back. Just *climb*."

It was a frantic, desperate scramble. Robert didn't know how he made it to the top. When he heaved himself over the edge, onto level ground, his half-healed leg was twitching uncontrollably. He lay flat on the ground, sobbing with fear and struggling not to retch.

"You can't stop there." Cam heaved at his shoulder. 'We have to get out of sight. Come on. On your feet."

Robert groaned. Zak caught hold of his arm and tugged him up, and the three of them began to battle their way through the stiff grass toward the shadows ahead. *Hide, hide, hide.* None of them said it, but the word was drumming in Robert's head with every step he took. There was no time for any other kind of thought. They had to get past the grassland and into the darkness beyond, underneath the great trees.

It took them ten minutes to reach the trees. As they drew near, the grass began to thin out. Eventually it disappeared completely and they were struggling through a vast, dank wasteland, roofed by arching branches as high as the sky.

The ground under the trees was cluttered with a labyrinth of dead leaves, heaped head-high, like old, damp carpets. Between the heaps, wet silt squelched underfoot, years deep and rotten. The air smelled of earth and decay, and the nearest tree trunk loomed above the leaf piles like a grim castle, several hours' walk ahead of them.

Cam plunged into the labyrinth as though she never meant to stop, but neither of them could keep up the pace she set. They were all breathless and desperate. The rotting silt sagged under them, and the piled leaves blocked their path.

When there was no way around, they had to clamber over the unstable, slithering heaps. After ten minutes of struggling, they were barely able to move.

"We can't go on," said Zak. "We need a rest."

Robert didn't want to stop. Not until he was too exhausted to think. Too exhausted to remember. But he knew Zak was right. They couldn't keep going forever.

"What are we going to do?" Cam snapped. "Go to sleep on top of the leaves? With a label saying, EAT ME?"

She looked up expressively, and Robert shuddered. It was obvious what she meant. They were hemmed in by the leaf piles, but not protected. Any bird that hopped close by—any dog, any hungry predator—would see them easily. They couldn't relax unless they found a hiding place.

"We'll have to stop sometime," Zak said. "And it's not going to be any different three hours farther on."

Robert nodded. There was only one way of hiding that he could see. "We'll have to burrow under the leaves."

Cam scowled. But she didn't argue. Crouching down, she began to part the dead leaves with her hands, making a space underneath the top layer.

"It stinks," she muttered.

It did. But there was no choice. Five minutes later, they were out of sight under the leaves, with their blankets wrapped tightly around them and their packs tucked close against their chests.

"OK. Let's get to sleep then," Cam said. She curled up, turning slightly away from the others.

"Not yet," said Zak. "There's something we have to do first."

Robert had no idea what he meant, but it was obvious that Cam knew. Her whole body tensed.

"We can't do it now," she muttered, without turning back. "Not in a place like this."

"The place isn't important." Zak was quiet but insistent. "We must do what's proper for Nate."

"Nate was a fool," Cam said. Her voice was indistinct, muffled in her blanket. "He shouldn't have been there on his own. He ought to have had someone watching out for trouble while he tied his pack."

Someone. Robert knew who that was.

"I should have been there," he said. The words almost choked him. "He knew I was worried about being slow across the stream, and he told me to go on ahead. But I should have stayed."

"It's not your fault," murmured Zak. "Nate was the hunter. He knew what to do. He should have *ordered* you to stay."

Robert shook his head. "He was my friend. He was trying to help me."

"He shouldn't have let that interfere," Cam said sourly. "He—"

She didn't finish what she was saying, because Zak interrupted her. "Begin," he said. This time his voice was harsh and full of authority.

For a second, Cam was very still. Then she began to speak in quite a different way, with a kind of awkward formality.

"Nate lived with us and now he is dead. We do not want to let him go, but we cannot bring him back by protesting or by grieving. We shall miss him."

"What will you miss?" said Zak.

There was a little pause. Then Cam said, "He was the best hunter that we had. He knew how to concentrate without being afraid."

Zak turned his head slightly, toward Robert. "And what about you? What will you miss?"

Robert didn't need to think. "He was my friend. He was always helping me."

"He noticed when people needed help," said Cam. "But he always did it without a fuss."

"He made his mind up carefully." Robert hadn't realized that before, but when he said it Nate came to life sharply in his mind. Thinking things over and then—when he had thought—making a firm decision. "He was sensible but he wasn't frightened of taking a risk."

Zak lay motionless, not speaking a word, while Robert and Cam remembered in turn. Nate seemed nearer and more real with every word they spoke, and the speaking held him there with them.

After a long time, there was silence.

Zak let the silence stretch out until it was almost too much to bear. Then he said, "Nate is dead now. We can't change that. We have to accept it and say good-bye to him. That is how it has to be."

"Good-bye, Nate." Cam's voice shook as she said it. "We shall miss you."

"Good-bye, Nate," said Zak. "We will remember you."

Robert closed his eyes. "Good-bye, Nate." He forced himself to say it, but he knew it wasn't enough. It was a moment before the right words came to him. When they did, he spoke them clearly into the darkness. "He was called Steven."

He had never said it out loud, but the name came easily, fitting his memory of Nate. Reminding him of how much he didn't know and now would never know.

"Good-bye, Steven," said Cam and Zak together.

Then they slept.

IV

into the dark

22

Lorn dreamed of frost and night.

She was wandering over bare ground so hard and cold that her feet stuck to the earth. Pulling them free stripped off the skin, layer by layer, until she was walking on raw flesh, but there was no feeling, because her legs were numb.

Gazing down she found that she could look into her own body. Through the transparent skin she saw ice crystals forming, blocking the arteries and clogging the muscle fibers. Her heart labored to pump the slow, thick blood and her lungs ached, drawing in air that froze the flesh inside.

Darkness ate at the edges of her consciousness, blurring her mind. The warm core of her body was breaking down. She opened her mouth to yell defiantly, or to call for help, but the ice invaded her throat, turning the soft flesh rigid and choking her. . . .

And then she woke.

She was in Zak's sleeping place, by the cavern entrance. That evening, without a word, the others had moved her blankets there. Twice, while they sat talking, she had gotten up to put the blankets back into her usual corner, but each time they had reappeared beside the mouth of the tunnel. In the end, she had given up and gone to sleep where they wanted her to be.

Waking now, she could feel the draft that seeped in under the bushes blocking the entrance. The cold air curled its way between the branches, and she knew, without thinking, that the temperature had dropped while she was asleep.

She put her face closer to the dark space and sniffed. Not frost. Not yet. But it was nearer than before. Even with her blanket, she was shivering. Very soon the frost would be there.

Pulling the blanket around her shoulders, she stood up and padded across to the brazier, walking close to the left wall of the cavern. The others were all huddled on the opposite side, to avoid disturbing the journey line. Lorn walked close beside the sticks that protected it, following it along the wall.

The four small stones had inched a little way farther down the line. Perdew and Bando moved them a short distance each day, and now they were about a quarter of the way along it. Crouching down, Lorn laid her hand over them. They were cold to touch, and she winced, imagining what it must be like outside. Even inside, it would be bitterly cold now, without the brazier.

And every day it would get colder.

She picked up the stones and cupped them in her hands to warm them. Bando was talking to himself as he slept. She could hear him mumbling disjointedly. Still holding the stones, she walked on down the cavern and stopped beside him, listening to pick out the words.

". . . Hello? Hello? . . . Is that—oh, hi, Cam! . . . Yes, it's me . . . it's Bando. . . . How are you doing . . . ?"

For a moment Lorn could almost hear Cam's distant, faint replies. The thought of it—the illusion—was too much to bear. She caught her breath painfully.

The noise woke Perdew. When he saw her standing there, he got up quietly and came to join her.

And Bando went on mumbling. "Great to hear your voice, Cam. How's things? . . . How far have you gotten? . . . What's it like?"

Very softly, through gritted teeth, Lorn said, "I can't bear it."

Perdew put an arm around her shoulders. "I dream about phone calls, too," he muttered. "All the time. And letters and e-mails. If we could just have one message—somehow—"

"But it's not going to happen, is it?" said Lorn. "We can't find out anything. All we can do is wait."

And all the time it's getting colder.

She moved her cupped hands again to warm the stones. And then, seeing Perdew watching her, she opened them to show him what she was holding. He shook his head disapprovingly.

"Put them back. Bando will go crazy if he wakes up and finds them gone."

"They were so cold," Lorn said.

But she turned back toward the line, looking for exactly the right place. When she found the little dents the stones had left, she began to lay them down. The red one first, and then the gray one and the yellow one.

When she came to the last—the black one—something made her hesitate. She weighed it in her hand reluctantly, looking down at the dent.

Then Perdew hissed at her. "Quickly! He's waking up!"

Lorn put the black stone down hastily, against her better judgment. But she wasn't fast enough. Bando heard Perdew's whisper, and he looked around and saw her.

"Leave the stones alone!" he shouted.

Lumbering onto his feet, he charged down the cavern toward her.

"They're all there," Lorn said soothingly. "Look."

But she hadn't been careful enough. The moment Bando saw the stones, he flew into one of his stupid, blind rages.

"The black one shouldn't be there! Can't you see? It's in the wrong place!"

He snatched it up and threw it furiously, as hard as he could. There was a *chink* as it bounced off the brazier, and it disappeared into the shadows.

Immediately Bando was horrified at what he'd done. He raced off down the cavern to get the stone back.

But they couldn't find it anywhere.

23

WHEN ROBERT WOKE, HE WAS STIFF AND COLD AND IT WAS already evening. Cam had wriggled out from under the leaves and she was gazing up at the sky.

"Look," she said, half under her breath. "It's the wires."

Robert pulled himself to where she was crouching. It was getting dark, but there was enough light to make out the thick, horizontal lines. The impossible cables they had seen at the end of the tree wall were high in the air above them, off to the right. They ran straight across the wasteland, from one concrete pillar to another.

"They go all the way," Cam said. "Right to the corner."

For a second, Robert didn't understand why she sounded so excited. Then he looked around and saw how dark and gloomy it was, and how the leaf piles blocked their view, in every direction. With nothing to guide them, they could have walked around in circles forever.

But they could rely on the wires.

They set out as soon as they had eaten, plodding patiently over the thick, wet silt. Their footsteps made no sound. After the intensity of the day before, the stillness and silence were like a dream, and they walked without speaking, deep in their own thoughts.

It was very slow. They took half an hour to reach the next concrete pillar and another hour to reach the one after that.

There was nothing but the pillars to mark off the time, and they walked on and on, until it was too dark to see.

Then they crawled under the leaves again, to sleep.

This time they didn't lie separately, in their own blankets. They had lost heat too fast that way. It was better to make a space that was big enough for all three of them. They used the blankets to line it and lay curled up together, lapped in fur and breathing each other's breath in a close, damp warmth.

As soon as they were settled, Robert became aware of a strange, low vibration coming through the earth. It surrounded him completely, as if he could hear the ground breathing, and his body vibrated to the same humming rhythm. It swelled and faded and swelled and faded, but it never disappeared altogether.

He was going to ask the others what they thought about it, but he wasn't quick enough. Before he could put the words together, their breathing changed and they were asleep.

BY THE SECOND DAY, HE KNEW THEIR BREATHING SO WELL THAT he could tell the different rhythms apart, with his eyes shut. He learned their smells, too, from all the time they spent curled up under the leaves. Cam sweated more than Zak, but beneath the sharpness of the sweat, her essential smell was fresh and sweet, like newly split wood. Zak was quite different. He smelled dry and cool, like fresh clay.

Gradually the three of them took on the colors of the earth. Their skins had been dirty before. Now the wet silt stained them a deep brown and their worn bat-leather tunics crumpled into soft folds, like veining on dead leaves. From three steps away, they were invisible, but Robert could locate the other two without looking, picking their individual scents out of the complicated mix in the night air.

They traveled in twilight and at dawn, in the dim hours of the day. When it was too dark to see where they were going, or too light to be safe, they wriggled in under the loose leaves and slept, gathering their strength again.

They never saw the sun. They were always surrounded by shadows and strange, indeterminate sounds. When they were up and traveling, they moved through a world without colors, full of dim shapes and indistinct, half-seen movements. They heard the *kiuuu* of the night bird high above them and the rustle of unknown creatures passing near at hand.

Lying under the leaf litter, they were wrapped in darkness, and the leaves moved all around them, nudging at their fur cocoon. Small, hard feet padded over its surface. Curious antennae intruded into any opening. Long, muscular bodies slithered past, rippling against the outside of the blankets. Every inch of the dark, barren ground had its own tenants, and Robert learned fast which of them had to be fought off with a quick jab of his spear.

He learned which of them to eat, as well.

There was no other food to add to the grain they carried. Nothing green grew around them, and they dared not try any of the fungi that clung to the dead leaves. To get enough food to keep them going, they had to hunt the creatures around them, spearing soft, wriggling flesh and cracking open hard, armored casings.

All the time—hunting or walking or sleeping—Robert was aware of the strange vibration growing stronger.

———

By the end of the fifth day, it couldn't be ignored. It hummed in the air when they woke before dawn, and they could feel it even when they were up and walking. It seemed louder with every step they traveled. They had to brace themselves against it when they rested at midday, and by evening their whole bodies were ringing with it. In the darkness it brought with it a bright, low light that flared and vanished suddenly.

They hardly slept at all that night. The humming filled their heads and buzzed in their brains. The strange light swept over the dead leaves, flooding everything with a cold brilliance that pierced even the top layers. Even inside the fur blankets. Robert saw Cam's shadowy face, with the eyes gleaming, and he knew that she was thinking the same as he was.

We're almost there.

The next day they reached the end of the park. The great trees stopped two hours before the end, but the metal bars went all the way, running through a green jungle of thorn vines and creepers, to a single concrete pillar in the far corner.

It was evening when they struggled through the last of the jungle and reached the foot of the pillar. Cam stood in the shadows, looking up at it.

"Bet there's a good view from the top," she said.

She had to shout now, to make herself heard. The vibrations had grown into a loud roar that came and went constantly, echoing in their heads and shaking their whole bodies. Its flaring light alternately dazzled them and plunged them into darkness, and the smell of it tainted the air they breathed.

The damp, green scent of the plants was overlaid by an acrid, metallic stench that filled their lungs and clung to the backs of their throats.

Robert gazed up at the pillar, trying to see it properly. It was lit from above by a steady, orange glow, but every few seconds the roaring swamped it with a burst of raw light that sent long shadows shooting around it.

Through the shadows the pillar rose into the sky, massive and unmoving. Vast loops of creeper snaked over the whole surface, spiraling one over another to the very top.

"I think we could get up there," Robert yelled.

Instantly Cam tucked her spear through the straps of her pack and began to climb, hauling herself from one ring of creeper to another. Almost immediately she was out of sight, lost among the dark leaves. Until the bright light flared. Then she was visible for a brief second, flattened against the pillar.

It was like watching a thunderstorm in slow motion. Sound and light came together, intense and overwhelming—but only for a moment. Then it was dark again, until the next flare. Each time, the light found Cam higher than before, but she was always still. As though she had jumped magically, without any effort.

Robert put his mouth to Zak's ear. "We'd better get going, too," he said.

Zak nodded and started to scramble up behind Cam. Robert waited a few seconds and then set off steadily after him, pulling himself through the dark. He froze whenever the light caught him, and that slowed him down and cramped his muscles into awkward positions. It was almost twenty minutes before he reached the place where Cam and Zak had stopped.

They were just below the very top, sitting side-by-side on a ledge where two strands of creeper had twisted together. As Robert hauled himself up to join them, they were staring out at what lay ahead, and he turned to follow their eyes.

He found himself looking into chaos.

The darkness was full of moving lights and swooping, sliding reflections—white, red, orange, yellow, green. The sound was beyond noise, forcing its way into his ears like a liquid and filling the air with choking fumes.

He "knew" what he was seeing. He had words for it. *Traffic. Road. Headlights.* But those words had nothing to do with the turmoil in front of him. He shut his eyes and put his hands over his ears.

The next time the noise died down, he looked again. Now everything was still under the eerie orange light. And running left and right in front of him, as far as he could see, was a long, shallow ridge of black ground, completely bare of vegetation. Its surface was as rough as a lava field. It sloped up gently and evenly to a narrow plateau and then fell away again on the far side.

Behind it, in the distance, was a high wall as tall as the pillar where they sat. And beyond that, far, far off and way up in the darkness, were huge rectangles of light, hanging against a flat backdrop of solid black.

Tilting his head back, Robert looked at the rectangles, forcing himself to see the patterns they made. Then he hunted for the structures that held them in place. Gradually he began to make out the hunched shapes of the gigantic, brick cliffs that rose up sheer beyond the lava field and the wall.

I know those houses. One of them is ours.

He went back to the rectangles and counted them, figuring out which were which. Which windows were his. When he was sure, he stared across at them, trying to think *home*. But his mind wouldn't do it.

When the next light came, he closed his eyes against it, and Cam leaned sideways, yelling into his ear.

"So you think we can get across there? How long do you reckon *that's* going to take?"

Robert waited until the light had passed. Then he opened his eyes and studied the black ridge ahead of them. "Twenty minutes? Half an hour? Depends how rough the surface is. It wouldn't take long if we could get a clear run at it."

If.

Looking sideways he saw Cam's wry smile. He saw Zak frowning at the vast shapes thundering past. *Car. Bus. Truck.*

The names were ridiculous. Cars and buses and trucks were made to fit people. People could drive them around or cross the road in front of them. These were storm machines, too big to see whole. Their shapes blurred in Robert's brain, hammering the same thought at him, over and over again.

We have to get past those. We have to get across.

After a long time, Zak tugged at his arm, pointing toward the ground. Cam was already disappearing down the pillar. For the last time, Robert looked across at the great wall and the lighted panes beyond it. Then he let himself off the ledge and began to climb down.

When they reached the bottom, they retreated a little way into the green jungle and crouched there, exhausted by the climb and the foul air and the incessant, ugly vibrations.

It was cold now—the coldest it had been so far. Once they'd

stopped climbing, Robert began to shiver. He looked around for a place to make a burrow, but the thorn vines were hard and jagged, and the ground was thick with creepers. Digging would take too long and use up too much energy.

Cam slid the bundle off her back and unrolled it, doling out the last of the grains she was carrying. They chewed without speaking, working at the grain until it was soft enough to swallow. When there was nothing left, they drank and refilled their shells with dew.

Robert sat back on his heels and looked at the other two, waiting for the next break in the noise. When it came, he said, "We have to cross. Otherwise this whole journey has been for nothing."

And Nate's death . . . But he didn't say it.

When the light flooded around them again, he saw that Cam was looking grim and unconvinced. But Zak was nodding.

"We should get a clear space in the middle of the night," he said, when he could make his voice heard. "But we need to plan it. We'll be completely exposed out there."

Robert thought of the night bird and shuddered. "Do we have to go at night? Maybe we could hitch a lift across on someone's shoe."

Neither of the others bothered to answer that. The moment the words were out, he knew himself that it would be stupid and dangerous to try.

"But it's *all* dangerous," Zak murmured. "Dangerous at night and dangerous in the day. Dangerous to go and dangerous to stay here. The world isn't made for people our size. It's just a question of which risks we choose."

Robert looked through the tangled plants around them, out

toward the orange glare and the bare, ugly space beyond the park. He let the roaring swell and die away three times before he answered.

Then he said, "OK, I'm choosing. We'll cross in the middle of the night. Tonight."

24

IT WAS A LONG, HARD WAIT. FOR THE FIRST FEW HOURS, THEY huddled together at the base of the pillar, enduring the noise, with the furs pulled around them like a tent to keep out the cold.

When the furs weren't enough, Robert began to hunt for reasons to move around.

"We could collect stones," he said, into one of the silences. "It would be good to have something to throw."

He didn't say why. Even mentioning the night bird seemed too much of a risk to take. But the others knew what he meant. Cam grinned and scrambled up, tugging her fur free. She began to scout around energetically, searching for stones that were small enough to carry.

Zak let her go. Then he said, "We can do better than stones. Look over there."

He pointed at the edge of the jungle, right by the start of the lava field. Something grimy and pale had snagged against the thorn vines. It hung in a damp, soggy mass, close to the ground.

Zak went across and began to tug at it, pulling off handfuls and working the shreds together in his hands. Robert had no idea what he was doing, but he went to help. While Cam stacked stones at the base of the pillar, he and Zak made a line of paper balls that dried quickly into small white missiles.

When they had made thirty or so, Zak fetched his batpack

and began to load it with a mixture of stones and paper balls. Then he rolled it up and roped it in a strange way, in a long, vertical sausage, with the top left open.

"It's good to have something that will catch the light," he said, in the next little silence. "You take some, too."

Robert still didn't understand, but he had enough faith in Zak to do what he said. He went to get his own batpack, bracing himself for the noise to start again.

It took longer than he expected. He had loaded the pack and was asking Zak how to roll it by the time the roaring came to drown out his voice. In the light, he and Zak looked at each other, thinking the same thing.

Cam had noticed, too. As soon as the sound died away, she started to count, measuring the seconds.

"One, two, three . . ."

She reached seventy-five before the next noise. And immediately after it was over, she began to count again.

"One, two, three . . ."

Until then Robert had barely noticed that the gaps were getting longer. That there were clear spaces now. But over the next couple of hours, as Cam counted, he heard the pauses lengthen gradually. She reached six hundred . . . seven hundred . . . a thousand. . . .

"We could have gotten across that time," she said then.

"Give it another hour," Zak murmured.

Robert leaned back against the pillar. He was very tired and the steady counting made him sleepy. For a while he dozed in snatches, listening to the same words over and over again.

"One, two, three, four, five . . ."

IN THE END, HE MUST HAVE SLEPT LONGER, BECAUSE HE WOKE suddenly and heard her saying, ". . . two thousand three hundred and eighty-four, two thousand three hundred and eighty-five, two thousand three hundred and eighty-six. . . ."

"It's enough," Zak said quietly, breaking into the counting. "There's plenty of time. All we need now is luck."

He stood up, hoisting his pack into position. Cam tied on the water shell and then he walked forward, past the pillar, under the high metal cables, and out onto the wide, open space of the lava field.

Robert held his breath, looking all around for movement. Everything was still. Zak scrambled forward over the rough black surface of the lava, making for a broad band of pale stone that ran across it.

Robert hadn't even noticed it before. But now, watching Zak head that way, he knew what it was. It marked the edge of a sheer drop. A cliff. Zak had to let himself down that precipice before he could even begin to climb the long, shallow slope of the lava ridge.

Zak didn't loiter. Glancing left and right, he began to run, leaping from one black mound to another. In a few seconds, he had crossed the level strip in front of them and reached the edge of the cliff. Kneeling down, he turned around and let himself over the edge. For a second Robert saw his fingers gripping the pale stone. Then he disappeared completely.

"Now we have to watch!" Cam said fiercely. She had a paper ball in one hand and a stone in the other. "Look at the sky—and count!" She began again, muttering the numbers under her breath.

Robert grabbed two stones and stepped out from behind the pillar, onto the edge of the lava field, to get a clear view of the sky. He scanned it from one side to another, backward and forward, watching for the dark, floating shape of the night bird.

There was nothing. The sky was empty.

After a moment, out of the corner of his eye, he saw a movement on the lava. Zak had appeared again, not running now, but toiling up the slope toward the top of the ridge. His shape was small and dim, but he still seemed frighteningly visible. He was the only moving thing in the whole great, bare space.

Robert peered harder into the sky, desperate not to miss anything. His throat was dry. He could hear Cam counting on, measuring how long Zak took to reach the top.

". . . two hundred and forty-three, two hundred and forty-four . . ."

When she reached seven hundred and four, she stopped. Robert glanced down and saw Zak outlined, horribly, against the yellow strip on top of the ridge. He broke into a jog and Robert held his breath, willing him not to stumble. Willing him to get over the plateau and into the shadows on the far slope.

In a few minutes he had done it. As he disappeared, Cam started counting again, scanning the sky as she chanted the numbers. When she reached seven hundred and four again, she stopped and let out a long breath.

"He must be there by now. It ought to be quicker going down the other side."

Robert nodded. "You go next. I'll keep you covered."

"OK." Cam gave him a long look. "Scared?"

"Of course," Robert said. There was no point in lying. "But we have to cross, don't we?"

Cam grinned. "Give me a hand with my pack then."

Robert fixed the shell for her. Taking her spear in her right hand, she stepped out quickly, as soon as he had tied the last knot. He watched her cross the first strip of lava. At the edge of the cliff, she turned and gave him a wave. Then she let herself over and dropped down out of sight.

Robert began to count silently.

One, two, three . . .

He heard Cam catch her breath sharply as she hit the ground at the bottom of the cliff, and he caught the clink of her pack as she stood up. But that was all. Her bare feet were silent on the rough surface of the lava.

. . . seventeen, eighteen, nineteen . . .

He was almost up to two hundred when he heard a stone rattle.

The noise came from beyond the crest, from the far side of the ridge. Was it Zak? Throwing stones?

There was another rattle. With a sudden flash of understanding, Robert stepped out of the shelter of the pillar and turned, looking back toward the great trees of the park.

And he saw the night bird.

It was floating above the trees, circling slowly closer as it surveyed the ground below. Glancing quickly over his shoulder, Robert saw Cam come into view, laboring up the dark side of the ridge. In two or three minutes she would be on the yellow strip at the top, completely exposed to the bird's great, piercing eyes.

He looked back and saw that it was closer now. He had to do something to distract it before it came right overhead. Hardly knowing what he was doing, he fumbled for the heap of paper balls and grabbed two of them. He threw them one after another, as hard as he could, aiming for the first strip of lava, before the precipice.

They were light but they carried well, and they landed exactly where he'd planned, one behind the other. Stones would have traveled farther, but no stone would have stood out like those two little dabs of white. And stones wouldn't have let him try what he meant to do next.

There was no sign that the night bird had seen anything. It was still moving in easy, questing circles. But it was almost over the fence now and, if he didn't distract it soon, it was sure to spot Cam when she crossed the yellow line. He bent and scooped up three stones from the pile.

He wasn't sure that he could hit the paper balls, but he had to try. Taking a deep breath, he threw one, two, three, very hard and fast. The first stone missed completely, but the second and the third hit the nearest paper ball, knocking it sideways.

Overhead, the night bird steadied, its attention caught. It was so high that Robert couldn't tell what it was watching. Out of the corner of his eye, he saw Cam, clear and vulnerable, scrambling up onto the plateau on top of the ridge.

Desperately he bent and scooped up more stones, throwing in a steady, even volley. One, two, three, four.

The night bird circled lower.

Let it see the paper, not Cam. Let it see the paper. . . .

Cold with terror, Robert bent and scooped and threw

again. One, two—The dark stones knocked the paper balls so that they moved erratically, jerking along.

And the bird dropped suddenly, coming down silent and huge out of the sky. It dropped—and Robert froze where he was, with his heart beating so fast that he almost passed out.

Let it see the paper. . . .

Halfway to the ground, the night bird leveled off and banked left, turning away. Rejecting the paper balls. It drifted back over the park, following the line of the great trees. Robert leaned against the pillar, weak and breathless, watching the easy, drifting shape disappear into the night.

When he turned back toward the lava field, Cam had disappeared, too. He had no idea whether she was safe under the cliff on the far side. His sense of time had gone completely. All he knew was that he had to set out right away, without waiting. Before he had time to think about the danger.

He tied the water shell onto his batpack and snatched up his spear. Stepping clear of the pillar, he ran out onto the open lava.

It was even rougher than he expected. Twice he missed his footing and nearly turned his ankle. It was impossible to look up without stumbling. He had to watch the ground all the time as he jumped and stumbled from one rough mound to another, horribly conscious of the sky above his head.

When he reached the edge of the cliff, he turned around to let himself down feet first, like the others. The bottom of the cliff was in darkness, and it was impossible to see how far he had to fall. He dropped blindly, landing on both feet and rolling over to break the impact.

Even so, it knocked the breath out of him. He crouched in

the shadow of the cliff until he had recovered and then set out up the slope. It curved away in front of him so that the top was hidden, and he found himself counting again, so that he had some idea of how he was progressing . . . *fifty-four, fifty-five, fifty-six . . .*

He had reached three hundred and fifty when he felt the ground begin to shake.

He knew, instantly, what it was. In a few seconds the vibration would turn to a roar. Then there would be a blaze of light. And then—

His mind went blank with terror. Instinctively he turned to run back into the shelter of the cliff behind him.

Just in time, he realized that he would never make it. He was already halfway up the slope, and running down again meant running right under the wheels of the storm machine. There was only one hope of surviving. Flinging himself to the ground, he shut his eyes and put his hands over his ears, lying still and flat against the rough, hard surface.

Please let it be a sober driver. Not a drunk going down the middle of the road. Please . . .

The shaking rose to a crescendo. Then the light came, flaring around him so that it lit up the space behind his closed eyelids. Why couldn't the driver see him? He was there, right there, in the middle of the road, right in front of the car. Why couldn't the driver *see?*

The light swept over him, and then he was plunged into darkness and engulfed by a gigantic roar. It was a hundred times louder than anything he had heard from the top of the pillar. It was all around him and in him, in every cell of his body. A searing wind rolled him over the rough ground, scorching his skin and filling his lungs with acrid, metallic fumes.

Don't let me die, like Nate. Don't let me die . . .

The storm machine went straight over him, suspended high in the air on its great, stinking wheels. He choked on the stench of rubber. A hail of sharp-edged grit bombarded every inch of his body, and his mouth was full of the taste of burning gas. Everything was blotted out, except the sheer, blind will to survive.

And then it was gone.

The wheels raced away into the distance, leaving a red afterglow behind them. Robert was weak and exhausted with terror and relief, but he knew that he couldn't recover, lying where he was. He had to get away from the foul, poisonous air that hung over him. Dragging himself up, he stumbled forward again. He was deafened by the noise, and his eyes were streaming so that he could barely see, but he blundered ahead, without waiting for them to clear. All he had to do was aim uphill and then keep going over the plateau.

Gasping and aching, he struggled on until he saw yellow under his feet. That meant he was halfway. He broke into a clumsy run and almost tumbled down the slope on the other side, heading for the cliff that had to be there. And the safe, welcoming shadow under it.

Cam and Zak were waiting there. They ran out of the shadow and caught hold of him, pulling him into shelter. As he collapsed against them, they took his weight and lowered him to the ground, letting him lie there and gasp for breath.

Zak put his face close to say something. Robert saw his lips move, but he couldn't make out the sounds. His ears were still full of the roar of the storm machine. Shaking his head to show that he didn't understand, he curled tighter, trying to stay where he was. He wanted to lie there at the bottom of the precipice until his head was clear and his body was rid of poison and fumes.

But Cam wouldn't let him. She caught hold of his arm and shook it fiercely, pointing up at the top of the precipice. Then she put her mouth right up to his ear and yelled at full volume, setting his head jangling.

"We have to find a hiding place. Before daylight."

He knew she was right. He knew he would die if he slept down there, on the cold ground. Someone would see him. Something would eat him. He would freeze to death. He had to move. . . .

Zak caught hold of his other arm, and he and Cam pulled together. Reluctantly, hardly conscious, Robert let them pull him up, onto his feet. He leaned forward against the cliff, with his head resting on the stone, and Cam held him steady while Zak scrambled up their backs and onto their shoulders to reach the top. For a second Robert felt the pressure of his bare feet. Then he was up, and Cam was yelling again.

"Climb on my shoulders! Hurry up!"

"Too heavy," Robert said drowsily. "You'll fall."

"Don't be stupid! I'm almost as big as you are!" Cam slapped at his face until he moved, and then she leaned against the cliff to take his weight, cupping her hands to give him a foothold.

The moment he was up, Zak was reaching down to take

his hands. Almost without effort, Robert found himself hoisted up onto the level ground at the top.

"Lie across my legs!" Zak bellowed into his ear.

Robert lay across them and Zak hung over the edge, reaching down to catch Cam's hands. She came up lightly, walking her feet up the face of the cliff.

"Nearly there," she said, as her head appeared next to Robert's.

He couldn't hear the words—but he saw her say them. And the seeing made him realize, for the first time, that it was getting light. It was nearly morning. The shock brought him to his feet, and he followed Cam and Zak as they ran across the last stretch of lava.

They threw themselves into a patch of ground covered with cropped, waist-high grass. Ahead was the great wall they had seen from the top of the pillar. They were so close now that it blocked out everything else. Robert stared up at it, still dazed and befuddled, wondering how they could possibly get past it.

Cam and Zak didn't waste time explaining. They just pulled him along to the right until they reached the end of the wall. Then they scurried around it, into the shadows behind.

And suddenly everything was different. They were past the lava and the coarse, sharp grass. Their feet were standing on loose, damp earth, with green leaves stretching all around them and overhead. The air was full of a sharp, clean smell that soothed away the stink of the storm machines. A bittersweet smell of . . . of . . .

It teased at Robert's memory, but he was too tired and confused to figure out what it was. He let Cam and Zak pull him in under the leaves, into safety.

They didn't bother to dig a hole. They just worked their way into the middle of the nearest clump of leaves, wrapped themselves tightly in their furs, and fell into a deep, heavy sleep.

25

ROBERT WAS ROUSED BY THE ROAR OF STORM MACHINES, SO
close that he woke sweating. He rolled over quickly, shrinking into the shelter of the wall behind him. His eyes were
tightly shut and his hands were over his ears. He was bracing
himself for the overarching darkness and the heat and the
scorching wind.

But they didn't come. The roars rose to a climax and then
faded, beyond the great wall that sheltered him. Slowly the air
cleared. He rolled over onto his back, opening his eyes.

And looked up into concentrated, singing color.

The sunlight filtered down through a canopy of orange,
richer than anything he had ever experienced or imagined. In
that first waking moment, he had no explanation for what he
was seeing. It was simply *orange* and he lay where he was,
staring up into the heart of it.

Twinned with the color—so close that they were the same
thing in his mind—came that fresh, sharp scent that had puzzled him the night before. It was familiar from way back, like
the smell of his own skin. Fresh and sharp and orange. He
liked it very much.

(But, somewhere at the back of his mind, he didn't *want* to
like it.)

He moved his head a fraction and saw a spear of pale green
running underneath the orange. Then another and another.
The singing color separated itself into broad rays that

snapped together with the light, bitter scent, making a sudden picture in his mind.

Marigolds.

As the word came to him, the orange above his head formed itself into great, rayed disks like a galaxy of secondary suns. Marigolds. Emma's flowers. Staring up at them, Robert knew exactly where he was. He was lying just inside the wall of his own front garden, on the one strip of ground not covered by concrete. Emma had always grown marigolds there, ever since she was old enough to scatter seeds into the earth.

He was home. If he had opened his eyes a few moments earlier, he would have seen his parents (*like two great skyscrapers*) sinking into their storm machines. That was the roaring that had woken him. The air was still full of the heat and exhaust fumes they had left behind.

Leaving his pack on the ground next to Zak and Cam, he wriggled between the thick, bristly marigold stalks to the edge of the bare earth. Pushing his head between two hanging leaves, he looked out at the long spread of concrete beyond.

Toward the house on the far side.

It was a mountain. The roughcast walls rose sheer and precipitous, set with sheets of glass like vertical glaciers. Dark trees flattened themselves against the base, and the peaked top stood clear and sharp against the sky.

Robert stared at it, appalled and mesmerized, trying to take in the mass of it, the vast, impregnable size. There was a rustle behind him, and Cam crawled out of the marigolds, stirring up a rush of scent as she brushed against the leaves.

"Is this the right place?" she said.

Robert nodded.

"So what are you going to do?" Cam said.

Until that moment, Robert had simply been staring, unable to think beyond that. Cam's question nudged him into looking at the huge cliff walls with different eyes. He noticed the flattened trees that grew around the base of the walls. He saw how their zigzag branches crawled up right to the foot of the lowest sheet of glass. They had scarlet fruit and thick, rounded leaves, like plates of armor.

Slowly an idea began to form in his head. He pointed at the top of the zigzag trees.

"That's the way up," he said.

"Not a bad climb," Cam said grudgingly. "But what are we going to do when we get up there?"

Robert wasn't sure enough about his idea to share it yet. He smiled and shrugged. "Let's deal with crossing the concrete first."

"Better do that before those cars come back," Cam muttered.

Cars. The word caught Robert off balance. Suddenly, in his mind's eye, he saw his mother's red Ford and his father's silver Peugeot. Not monstrous storm machines, but ordinary, familiar cars. They had driven straight past him, while he lay in the marigolds. Too small for them to see.

And when the cars left, it was almost time to set out for school. Which meant that, any moment now—

Crash!

The noise of the back gate came like an explosion. And then the sound of feet, shaking the ground. And the deep, creaking whirr of bicycle wheels.

He put his face down on the earth and blocked his ears. He wasn't ready to watch Emma's giant feet go striding past. He wasn't ready to gaze up and see her looming against the sky, a hundred times taller than he was.

When everything was quiet, he lifted his head and saw Cam watching him.

"Let's find something to eat," he said gruffly, before she could speak.

THEY BREAKFASTED ON MARIGOLDS. ZAK SWARMED UP THE bristling stalks and hung like a monkey, holding on with his legs and tugging at the orange petals until they came away with a jerk. They were as big as the blades of oars. Robert found that the only way to eat them was to chew until they were soft and then scrape the pulp off the fibers with his teeth. The taste was strong and strange, but there was nothing else, and he knew that they were safe to eat.

Marigold rice. Marigold buns. Petals in the salad. There was no escape from them. Emma found a new recipe almost every year.

He chewed doggedly, eating as much as he could stomach. Then Zak said, "It's going to rain."

He was right. Within a few moments, the light had dulled, and heavy, isolated drops began to fall through the marigold petals and trickle down the long, hairy stems.

"At least we've got some water to drink," Cam said wryly. "And we can fill the shells while we're waiting for it to stop."

But it didn't stop. An hour later it was still raining hard.

"We might as well get going," Robert said. "We're going to get just as wet sitting here."

Cam grimaced and picked up her spear. "At least the rain's

good cover. No one's going to stand around looking over the garden wall."

Zak didn't even comment. He just slung his pack onto his back and set out across the concrete.

It was hard going. The surface of the concrete was rough enough to make walking difficult, and there was no shelter of any kind. They were totally exposed to the rain, and within minutes they were drenched.

Their packs soaked up the water. The falling rain slid straight over them, but when the drops hit the concrete they splashed up again, like fountains, and the splashes found their way into the packs from underneath. They soaked into the furs, weighing them down so that the packs dragged backward. Robert had to put his head down and lean into the rain, just to keep going.

It ran into every groove and depression in the concrete. Most of the time they were wading through ankle-deep water. Robert's feet went numb and his bones ached with the cold, but he knew it would be crazy to stop. He kept moving mechanically, with his eyes fixed on Cam and Zak ahead of him and the dark, zigzag trees in the distance.

It took them two hours to reach the trees. By that time, they were all shivering and chilled to the bone. They ran the last few steps and dived into the shelter of the branches.

Under the trees the ground was dry and dusty, and there was a layer of crisp, dead leaves covering the concrete. The three of them stripped off everything except their tunics and spread the fleeces and furs on the dead leaves to dry. Behind the trees the wall was warm and solid, and they huddled against it, crouching close together and pulling more leaves around their bodies, to keep in the heat.

It was a long while before anything happened.

When it did, Robert was dozing, leaning back against the rough surface of the cliff. Cam nudged him suddenly, almost knocking him over.

"Who's that?"

He woke to see black shoes rising like walls in front of him in the half-light of the evening. Black cloth stirred the air above them, and Robert had a confused impression of metal and rubber whirling past and water splashing up around them.

Before he could think *Emma,* there was a scraping noise and then a thud, and she was through the back gate with her bicycle. Robert stood up, scattering dead leaves. He was shaking so much that he could hardly speak.

"The others will be back in half an hour or so," he said, fighting to keep his voice steady. "I'm going to climb up now. Take care of my pack for me."

Cam looked startled. "Aren't we coming, too?"

Robert couldn't bear the thought of that. "I'll call if I need any help."

Cam sighed impatiently, but Zak put a hand on her arm. "Let him be," he said.

Robert pulled himself into the nearest tree, finding footholds in the bark and scrambling up to the first branch. When he was safely up, he called down to the others.

"Pass up my spear."

They did it without comment, standing on tiptoe to lift it

above their heads. Robert leaned down and drew it up into the tree. It was cumbersome to carry, and it made climbing awkward, but it was vital to his plan. He went on working his way upward, maneuvering it around the jagged side branches, until he reached the first of the round, scarlet fruit.

They were almost as big as his head, and it took him several attempts to discover the best way of spearing them. Three or four went tumbling down to the ground before he caught the knack of stabbing them and the sharp twist that would break the stalk.

When he managed to spear one, he used both hands to work it past the metal point and down onto the shaft. Then he aimed at another. Three of the fruit filled the spear, from top to bottom.

They were so heavy that they pulled him off balance when he tried to climb again. He had to push the spear up ahead of him and lodge it safely before he could scramble up to the same level. It was hard work, but he kept going, getting nearer and nearer to the glass sheet at the top of the tree.

Cam and Zak called up to him from below.

"Are you all right?"

"Do you need any help?"

Their voices were thin and distant, muffled by the leaves. Robert shouted back, to reassure them, but his voice was drowned out by a sudden roar and a burst of light. Peering between the branches, he saw the glaring headlights of a storm machine. *Mom—*

The light was so dazzling that he almost fell. He closed his eyes and clung tightly to the nearest branch with his left hand. Through his eyelids he saw the first blinding glare change to a gentler red, and he turned his face away from the foul-tasting gases that billowed toward him.

As soon as the lights went out, he began to climb faster, desperate to reach the top before the second machine arrived. The spear had slowed him down more than he had expected, and he was beginning to worry whether he would make it in time.

Just before the top of the tree, a white ledge jutted out of the cliff. Robert pushed the spear up onto the ledge and hauled himself after it. It was hard to keep a foothold. The ledge sloped downward, and the surface was wet and slippery. He had to wedge his feet precariously against a branch that straggled up over the ledge to touch the glass.

Almost as soon as he was in position, the space beyond the glass was flooded with sudden yellow light. It opened up in front of his eyes, completely familiar—and grotesquely strange.

Mountainous crimson shapes—too huge to be chairs—towered up toward a vast, glowing globe. A long, raised surface gleamed with reflected light, like a polished tennis court. Patterns of red and blue and green meandered into endless space across the floor.

Home . . .

There was no time to make sense of it. A tall shape was moving quickly toward the window, monstrous as a moving hill—but with a familiar tilt to the shoulders. He scrambled closer to the glass, pressing his face against it. Feeling his heart lift. It was . . . it had to be—

The figure took another step, so that the light caught it full on. Robert saw a vast, coarse face, blurred out of shape. The bones themselves seemed to have bloated so that they lost definition. He knew who it was, even through all that. He recognized her.

But . . . big was *different.*

His eyes homed in on things that should have been insignificant. The lip grooves. The hairs that crawled over the mottled skin. The cavernous nostrils, large enough to take his head—

It was worse than he had ever imagined, even in the lowest moments of the journey. But he knew who she was. He *knew*. Pushing the images away—shutting off the part of his mind that was yelling *Ogre!*—he lifted up the spear with its load of brilliant, scarlet fruit. Holding it in full view, he waved it furiously to attract her attention. And he yelled, as loudly as he could.

"Mom! *Mom!*"

The vast face twisted into a gigantic grimace. The great mouth turned awry, the neck tensed into ropes, and she came across the room in two strides.

He yelled again, ignoring the message of her expression. Telling himself there was no way he could read a face that size. "Mom! It's me! Robert!"

It—*she*—bent forward until the face was too close for him to see it whole. The open mouth gaped level with his eyes, and he shouted into the great red throat.

"Mom!"

The head went up and out of view as the figure straightened. Now all he could see was a huge, thick-fingered hand, reaching for the window fastenings. Suddenly he realized what danger he was in.

"Mom! Don't—!"

He sidestepped quickly, dropping the spear and bending to grab at the branch below him. But he couldn't move fast enough. The window swept open, catching the top of his head and knocking him off his feet. And the great fingers flapped toward him, nails outward, flicking him away. As they crashed into him, he heard a deep rumble, sharp with disgust.

Such a kind woman. That was what people said about his mother. But she flicked him away with a single sharp movement of her hand, and he fell down and down, with his body curling automatically, his face tucked in under his raised arms.

Down and down, with the branches of the tree catching at him so that he snagged and fell, snagged and fell, all the way into the darkness.

26

LORN WOKE TO FIND BANDO KNEELING BESIDE HER, GAZING into her eyes as they opened. His face was so close that she screamed before she could stop herself.

Instantly Bando's face crumpled. He patted desperately at her arm. "Don't cry, Lorn. Don't cry. I was only checking . . . I was only wondering—"

"Checking *what?*" She sat up, shaking. "Couldn't you even wait till I was awake?"

"But I thought you might not . . . I mean . . . I didn't know—"

He was babbling now, shuffling away backward on his knees with his hands held up in front of his face, as though to ward something off. His whole body was shaking in a way that Lorn had never seen before.

"Don't be silly," she said. More gently this time. "You know I'm not going to hurt you. What's the matter?"

"Nothing. It's nothing. I just—"

He was like a picture of someone being pulled apart. Lorn could feel how much he wanted to speak to her. But there was something holding him back. Something very powerful. Her instincts whispered, *danger, danger,* and for a second she was overwhelmed by a vast feeling of helplessness.

I can't cope with all this stuff. I can't keep coping. . . .

And then the power kicked in and she was calm. She crossed her legs and sat up straight, beckoning Bando toward her.

He came, as she had known he would. That was part of the power. On his hands and knees, he shuffled back to her place by the tunnel. She stared at him until he looked up and met her eyes.

Then she said, "Why can't you tell me, Bando? What's stopping you?"

His eyes wavered, but she held them, willing him to speak. The word came very slowly, as though she had dragged it out of him.

"Zak—"

Before, that name would have been enough to warn her off. But now, with the power so strong, it gave her the password that she needed.

"Why were you staring at me, Bando?" she said. "You can tell me. I sleep in Zak's place now."

Bando's eyes slid away sideways and his voice came reluctantly. But he answered.

"I wanted to see if you were alive," he said. "You have to stay alive, because I can't remember what to do. Not without Cam and Zak."

Something dark stirred at the bottom of Lorn's mind, and only the power kept her steady.

"What's in your head?" she said. "What are you remembering?" *We don't speak about the past. Time goes forward, but never back.* She broke the taboo as easily as a paper chain. "Tell me, Bando."

His mouth began to tremble. "Winter," he said. "Winter. It's very cold, Lorn. It's so cold—and there's death. And things I have to do. But I don't know how without Cam and Zak. Will you tell me, Lorn?"

Winter.

The dark fear swelled in the bottom of Lorn's mind, and she knew that winter was at the core of it. But the rest was lost in Bando's scrambled brain, and she knew better than to try to bully him. Already there were tears glinting in his eyes. If she pressured him any harder, he would withdraw into silence, huddling into a corner and blocking out everything.

She had no right to do that. She slept in Zak's place now, and it was her job to help the others get by.

She stood up and held out her hand, beckoning to Bando to stand up. Leading him to the side of the cavern, she stopped halfway along the journey line and crouched down to draw in the dust with her finger. Right over the line, at the midpoint, she made the shape of a small house with a door and a pitched roof.

The colored stones—only three now—were a little way short of it. She nodded toward them.

"Move them on, Bando," she said. "They've reached Robert's house."

Bando knelt down, breathing hard with concentration. His fingers closed around the red pebble. Cam's stone. Carefully he slid it along the line until it was beside the house. He went back for the gray one and picked it up to brush away some crumbs of earth.

"Zak," he said. He laid it carefully on the other side of the house.

"Now Robert," said Lorn.

She was expecting Bando to move the yellow stone, too, but he didn't. He picked it up and held it out to her.

"You can do him," he said. "You like him, don't you?"

Lorn held out her hand, and he dropped the stone into it, so that it lay heavy and cool in the cupped palm. *Yes,* she thought. *Yes, I like him. Better than anything in the world.* She wanted, foolishly, to slip the yellow stone down inside the bloused top of her tunic, so that it lay against her skin. She wanted to keep it there, safe in the heat of her body, until the thornbushes were pushed out of the tunnel mouth and Robert himself—the real Robert—came crawling back into the cavern.

The longing was so powerful that her fingers were already closing around the stone, and she was looking left and right for something else to use on the journey line. There must be another small object that would do. The stones were only counters. It wouldn't matter if she changed one.

"Lorn?" Bando said. "What are you doing? Is something wrong with Robert?"

The stone was heavy in Lorn's hand. Special. Different from all other stones.

"Nothing's wrong," she said gently. And she leaned forward and placed the yellow stone carefully in the very middle of the house.

She saw that she had drawn the house to fit it. The square space under the pointed roof was exactly the right size. As she placed the stone in position, the power took over, and she pressed down, pushing the stone right into the ground and smoothing the loose soil over the top. When there was nothing to be seen except the neat lines of the house, she sat back, brushing the earth off her fingers.

"Robert's home," she said.

27

HE WAS CURLED UP IN FUR, LYING ON SOFT, DRY LEAVES. THE air around him was warm and damp with his breath, and there was no pain.

"Open your eyes," Zak said.

He didn't want to.

"Open your eyes."

It was easier to go on lying there, closed around by his own stillness, feeling the silky strands of fur against his skin. Zak's words pushed at the walls of his little, safe cocoon, and he resisted them, closing his mind to their meaning.

Zak began to hum. It was a quiet, deep sound without words, rising and falling like a slow pulse. There was nothing threatening in it. Nothing to fight. It was simply a movement of the air that drifted gently over the ground, rising and falling, rising and falling, on and on and on. . . .

After a long time, Zak said, "Robert."

It was the first time he had ever spoken the word. His voice was as soft as thistledown, but it carried authority. It had to be answered.

"I'm not Robert. You were right and I was wrong. Give me another name."

Speech was an effort that hurt his face and his neck and his ribs. And once he was aware of the hurt, his whole body began to clamor for attention, every inch of it sore and aching.

But the physical ache was trivial, was nothing, compared to

the pain in his mind. It swelled up like a vast, black wave, too big to comprehend. It swept toward him out of some deep place, ready to overwhelm him.

"You have a name," Zak said. "Open your eyes, Robert."

"No. I can't be Robert."

"There's no alternative now. If you aren't Robert, you're nothing. No one."

"I—"

The black wave was high in the air now, about to swamp him. He had come to the place where he should have been at home. He had stepped out of hiding, just as he was. And he had been swept aside, like a piece of rubbish. He wanted to lose that knowledge, to be a new person.

"There is no new person," Zak said relentlessly. "You have made your choice already. Tell me your name."

My name is Robert Doherty. He formed the words in his mind and knew that they were true. Turning to face the great dark wall of water, he looked straight into it and let it flow over him and around and through him, until it was as present and invisible as the air he breathed.

Then he opened his eyes.

"I am Robert," he said.

He reached out with both hands, through the fur, not knowing what he was reaching for, but knowing beyond question that it was the right movement.

Beyond the fur, his hands were cold for a second and then other hands closed around them, holding them hard. Zak gripped his right hand and Cam held his left, and the two of them said his name together—"Robert."

And he threw his head back and shouted, like a wild creature, like a child without language, letting out the noise that was inside him, making a sound that was without meaning because it meant everything, all that he knew and felt, all that he was.

His own, real sound.

AFTERWARD THEY SAT CROSS-LEGGED UNDER THE ZIGZAG TREE, looking out into the twilight.

"Big people don't see us," Cam said. "When they look straight at us, something goes wrong. What they see is—" She shrugged and spread her hands, letting the sentence die.

Robert considered his answer, choosing the fewest words, because every one was painful to speak. "But you let me come here. You came with me."

"Yes," Zak said.

Cam nodded, agreeing. Letting him know that it was no mistake.

Robert chose more words. "You knew it would end like this?"

He heard the answer in their stillness. Of course they'd known. All the time, all through the journey, they had known what was waiting for him. They had brought him here deliberately.

"Why me?" he said.

"You have the strength," Cam said. "You're clever and determined. And you're . . . big enough."

He didn't understand. He thought she meant something abstract, to do with his mind or his character. While he was still trying to make sense of it, Zak spoke, without looking at him.

"There is a critical size. Most of the others are too small to make it through the winter. Their body mass isn't big enough to retain the heat."

Robert stared at him. "What are you talking about?"

Cam took a long breath. "Perdew will die when it freezes. So will Annet and Dess and Tina. Bando will probably make it through. He's the biggest of us all and he's lasted three years now."

"And . . . Lorn?"

"Lorn will die first," Zak said. "She's very small."

Robert closed his eyes, remembering the feel of her body under his hands when he'd grabbed her in his burrow. The narrow, fragile wrist. The little bones. The delicate, busy hands. *No. Not Lorn . . .*

But his denial couldn't stop it being true. They were real people in a real world. And death was real, too.

"Do they . . . know?" he said. It was hard to speak the words.

Cam avoided his eyes. "They all know that some people die every winter." She turned her head away.

"They don't know that it's predictable," Zak said. "That it's as simple as adding up numbers. If you're too small, you die when the temperature goes below freezing for more than a couple of hours."

"Why can't they stay by the brazier?" Robert said quickly. "If they stay in and keep warm—"

"Then they starve." Zak's voice was gentle. Full of pity.

Robert had a blurred sense that he hadn't understood properly, that the pain was slowing his mind. "But we've been collecting food for the winter. Working hard."

"Come *on,*" Cam said harshly. "You've seen the supplies. Did you ever think there was going to be enough for everyone? For the whole winter?"

"I thought—"

He was going to protest that he had. That he'd assumed—

But it wasn't true. As soon as she said it, he knew that it had always been there, deep in his mind. *It won't work. They'll never get enough.* His mind had shied away from doing the calculations but, now he thought about it, the shortfall was obvious. They ate well over three-quarters of the food they collected. Had to eat it, to keep going.

"So Lorn and Dess and the others . . ." Robert was working it out as he said it. "They're collecting supplies they'll never eat? Because the cold's going to kill them off first?"

Zak nodded calmly. "But if they didn't collect, *no one* would make it through the winter. Even those who are big enough can't afford to go outside too often. And they can't collect a whole winter's food supply. Not on their own."

"So the small ones help the big ones to survive?" Robert looked down at his own thick, strong wrists and flexed his big, square hands. "That's horrible. That's exploitation."

"The alternative is—everyone dies," Zak said. "Is that better?"

"But they ought to know! They ought to have a choice!"

"They do know," Cam said dully. "In a way. They're not stupid. But they think that *if* they're careful, *if* there's enough to eat, *if* they keep up the fire—They think that something will happen to help them cheat death."

Only you can't cheat death. Not when you are nothing and no one. When you are too small to be seen. Too small to count.

Robert's mind ran in circles, like a hamster in a wheel. "Why can't we move into a house? It would be warm enough there."

"And what would we eat?" Zak said sarcastically. "Or do you know a house where they store the food at floor level? Have you ever tried climbing plastic or polished wood? What about cats and traps and feet?"

"There's no way out," Cam said. "No magic bullet. I've been trying to find one for three years now, and there isn't an answer. We just do the best we can."

There was a sick, sour taste in Robert's mouth. "I was better off not knowing. Why did you have to tell me?"

"Because there has to be a leader," Zak said. "Someone who knows how things really are."

"You've got Cam for that," Robert said bitterly.

Cam looked at him hard for a moment and then turned her head away. Zak put an arm around her shoulders.

"Over time, everyone gets smaller," he said softly. "Even those who start out big enough. Cam's had a good run, but she's not going to make it this winter."

Robert was too stunned to answer.

"There has to be a leader," Cam said, in her familiar, practical voice. With her head still turned away. "People need someone to keep them going. And it works. It's good in the cavern, isn't it? Even for people who are going to die. But I can't do it anymore. We need another leader. Someone who knows the truth. Who understands that no one's going to come swooping out of the houses to rescue us—that they don't even see us."

It was like being offered a monstrous weight to carry.

Robert saw what it would mean—the work and the responsibility and the loneliness—and his whole mind recoiled.

"Isn't there someone else? Can't Zak—?"

"No," Zak said. "It has to be you."

Everything they'd said was ringing in Robert's brain. *If you're too small, you die.... There has to be a leader.... No one's going to come swooping out of the houses to rescue us....*

"It's too hard," he said.

"It's how things are," said Zak. "This isn't a game, Robert. It's real."

Real ...

The word dropped into the center of Robert's brain. He sat and thought about Lorn and Bando and the others in the cavern. About food and fire and the winter on its way. About Nate.

It was all solid and real in his mind. As solid as his own body sitting cross-legged on the ground. He felt the weight of the job he was being given, but he felt his own strength, too—and he knew he could do it.

It was all real....

He made himself remember his own reflection in the restroom mirror, high above the clouds. That was the image he had been clinging to all this while. *I'm still the same person.... I'm still me.... I'm going to find a way of getting back to what I was.*

But what was a reflection? Just light bouncing off a glass surface. Something as thin and insubstantial as a photograph. Deliberately he opened his mind and let it float away.

I am here now, he thought. *This is the only place where I can change things.*

Cam and Zak had both turned toward him, and he caught their familiar scents, carried on the night air. He was acutely aware of the roaring noises and the lights and the dappled shadows of the round, shiny leaves over his head.

"All right," he said. "I'll do it."

Zak gave him a strange look. "What will you do?"

"Whatever it takes," Robert said. "Anything."

Zak raised his eyebrows and Robert said it again, carefully this time. Knowing that he was committing himself to more than he could see in advance.

"I'll do whatever it takes."

Cam stood up briskly. "OK, then. We'd better get going. It's a long way back to the cavern. Are you ready?"

An hour ago Robert would have obeyed without thinking, because he was used to Cam being in charge. But things were different now. He looked across the dark concrete and then backward, up at the house.

"Let's think a bit," he said. "It took us a long time to get here. Before we go back, we ought to make sure there really isn't anything we can do."

"To make them see us?" Cam looked scornful. "I thought you'd gotten it into your head. They're not *going* to see us. We're too small."

"There must be something." Robert frowned.

"Oh sure," Cam said sarcastically. "Maybe we could build a microscope and stand underneath it. How about that?"

One of Zak's eyebrows went up, echoing her question. At that instant a little breeze blew across the concrete, carrying the bitter scent of the marigolds—and an idea flowered suddenly in Robert's head.

233

Not a microscope, but maybe something they'd be sure to see. Something big enough . . . He looked toward the marigolds and took a long, deep breath, drinking in the smell. *If we could make a picture* . . .

The image in his head was bold and flamboyant and risky. But it might work. And if it did, there would be a chance of saving Lorn and the others—instead of going back to watch them die.

He looked up at Cam. "We're not going yet," he said. "There's one more thing we can try."

28

WHEN HE TOLD THEM WHAT HE WANTED TO DO, CAM WAS horrified.

"That's crazy. You want us to slog back across the concrete, and work all night, and use up all our energy—just to make some kind of *picture?*"

"It's not just a picture," Robert said. "It's a chance to make a difference. Don't you see—" Running out of words, he spread his hands, trying to get Cam to share his feeling of urgency. Of opportunity.

She looked scornful, but Zak shook his head at her. "He has to do it, Cam. Don't try to stop him."

Cam still didn't look convinced, but she followed the other two as they set out to walk back to the marigolds.

It was a darker journey this time. Retracing their steps took them under the nearest storm machine. Its huge body made a gloomy roof high over them as they trudged from one end to the other. The stench of old exhaust fumes lingered in the air, and the ground was dirty and stained with oil that clung to the soles of their feet.

It was a relief to come out at the far end, even though that left them exposed to the open sky. They jogged the rest of the way, with their packs bouncing and their greasy feet slithering on the hard surface. Tumbling into the shelter of the marigolds, they leaned against the solid stalks, breathing in their strong, clean scent.

In the dark the flowers had closed up, like umbrellas. Cam looked up at them for a moment or two. Then—without saying anything—she began to climb, scrambling up the nearest stalk with her spear tucked behind her bundle.

"She's going to help, then," Robert muttered.

"Of course." Zak sounded amused. "Did you think she'd let you down?"

The stem began to shake as Cam sawed away at the top of it. A few moments later, she called, "Watch out!"

Zak pulled Robert out of the way and the flower head fell suddenly. It hit the ground not with a crash but with a soft, disconcerting bounce. Lying next to them, it was as tall as they were.

"We'll drag it," Robert said. "We should be able to manage that together."

Zak looked at him. Then he looked at the strip of open concrete between the marigold bed and the storm machine.

Robert knew what he meant. This was only the first flower. There were dozens more, and each one would have to be moved separately. Across the open space.

He looked back at Zak and shrugged. "Everything's dangerous for people our size," he said. "It's just a question of which risks you choose."

Zak grinned and bent down to take hold of the marigold.

They worked all night, taking turns to climb the stems and cut off the flower heads. The two on the ground dragged the flower heads over the concrete and into the shelter of the storm machine. There were thirty-four altogether, and they cut and moved every single one.

Under the storm machine, they pulled the flowers to pieces.

236

Cam and Robert took the big outer petals and laid them out in concentric circles on the stickiest patch of oil. They walked around and around in the dark, putting them in position to make a pattern they could hardly see. Off to one side, Zak sat patiently, working at what remained of the flower heads, stripping off all the green parts to leave pads of small, brown florets.

By the time all the large petals were laid out, the dark was already thinning. Robert glanced toward the garden beyond the storm machine, narrowing his eyes and trying to judge how late it was. There wasn't much time left. And he had another flower to find.

"I'm starving," Cam said. "And exhausted."

"Eat some marigold petals. We can spare a few." Robert heard his own voice, sounding as brisk as hers did when she was giving orders. He was beginning to understand what it meant to be focused. To see the thing that needed doing and concentrate all your energies on getting it done. He nodded at the pattern of petals and the little, dark pads that Zak had made. "You finish off here. I have to get the last thing. I should be back in an hour or so."

As he set off, he was praying that his mother hadn't been seized with a sudden desire to tidy the garden. The marigolds were grown deliberately, but this other plant was a weed. An intruder that scrambled along the bottom of the side wall, rooting in its crevices.

Stinko. Pimple-head. Poke plant.

It was so small and insignificant that he would never have noticed it on his own. But Emma had spotted it. For years, from the moment she had discovered its name, she'd taunted him with its soapy smell and the dirty feel of its leaves.

Louse-top. Pong-weed. Sneak-in.

When he was younger, it used to madden him. Time after time, he had tugged up all the horrible red stalks, trying to root out the whole plant. But it always had sneaked back somehow. In the end he'd given up, hating the insignificant, insistent flowers and the rampant way they spread.

He toiled across the concrete, keeping a nervous eye on the sky. It was just after dawn, and the world was made up of dim shapes that gradually became clearer as he went.

He was a dozen steps away from the side wall when the soap smell hit him. Peering ahead, he made out the ugly straggle of leaves and stalks that spread along the edge of the concrete and up the wall, clinging in any crack that offered a roothold.

As he walked forward, he began to notice the colors. The green of the delicately cut leaves shaded into a deep crimson. The stalks were blood-red, rich against the earth colors of the brick wall. Their tiny hairs caught the light like threads of crystal, and dozens of long, pointed seedpods stabbed at the air with hummingbird beaks.

It took him by surprise. For a second—looking from leaf to stalk to seedpod—he forgot why he had come. He just stood and stared at the intricate, graceful plants spread out along the wall.

Then he remembered that what he needed was a flower.

He knew that most of the flowers were gone before the marigolds came, but all he needed was one. One last, late bloom among the pointed seed heads. His eyes traveled around the leaves and over the stalks, searching. Surely there would be one left.

It took him almost ten minutes to spot it. It was right in the corner of the wall, growing with its back to him, so that he only glimpsed the pink petals behind the hairy swell of the base. It wasn't until he'd struggled all the way around to the other side that he saw the flower properly.

It was stunning.

Five rounded petals spread into a classic flower shape, bigger than his head. Their fine, clear pink was streaked with white lines converging into the luminous green center. Out of that center, from the very heart of the flower, rose a cluster of translucent stems, each one tipped with brilliant orange pollen.

He stood and stared at it.

It's beautiful.

Emma had taunted him with flowers like that a hundred times. And he had believed what she had said, grabbing at them with rough, angry hands. Crumpling them into nothing and ripping them out of the earth. He had hated them because he had never *seen* them properly. Because—

Because he was too big.

He stared at the flower for a long time. Then he hooked the shaft of his spear around the stalk and pulled the stem down until he could hold the top. Using the spear blade carefully, he cut through the arched stem, leaving the cut piece long enough to wind through the strings of his pack. With the flower nodding above his head, he set out back to the others.

By that time, the sun was up, and that short walk was the most terrifying part of the whole journey. He was completely exposed, with the pink flower waving over his head to draw attention to him as he moved.

When he finally reached the shelter of the storm machine, Cam shot out and dragged him underneath.

"Are you insane?" she said. "What took you so long?"

"It's all right." Robert slipped off his pack and worked the flower stem loose. "I found one."

The pink flower was pitifully small next to the big swirl of marigold petals. Looking at the two of them together, Robert felt a shiver of uncertainty. He imagined Emma's eyes skimming over the picture they'd worked so hard to make, and he felt—silly.

She'll never understand. . . .

But it was the only chance there was. He had to try.

Bending down, he laid the pink flower on the ground beside the pattern of marigold petals, choosing a spot where the leaked oil was thick and dark, so that the colors showed up clearly.

He was just in time. As he stood up again, there was a loud thud, and the ground quivered with the tread of heavy feet.

"They're coming," Zak said softly.

Mom and Dad . . . the cars . . .

"Which one goes first?" Cam hissed.

Robert knew it didn't matter. In a couple of seconds, both machines would be on the move. There was no chance of getting away from them.

"Just get *down!*" he snapped.

As they threw themselves flat onto the concrete, the high roof over them creaked and sagged. There was a loud, metallic crash. Then another one.

They're both inside the cars, then . . .

Robert had been anticipating all that. It was the fumes that took him by surprise. As the engine started up above them, the puff of exhaust hit the great wall of slatted wood behind it and billowed back into the space where they were sheltering. They were engulfed in clouds of suffocating, poisonous smoke.

The next moment, the storm machines were on their way, in a burst of heat and stink and noise. Blinded and choking, Robert and Cam and Zak dragged themselves up and stumbled toward the side of the garden with their eyes streaming. Trying to reach clean air before they had to breathe again. They didn't stop moving until they were close to the bottom of the side wall.

That wasn't part of Robert's plan. He wanted to be standing still and upright next to the pink flower, not doubled over and gasping for breath. He struggled to straighten up and stagger back into position, but there wasn't time. He was still coughing when the ground began to quiver again.

There was a loud scrape beside the cliff wall of the house. The slatted wood swung away from him, its base catching on the concrete. Robert looked up and saw the huge, rounded toes of Emma's black school shoes moving toward him.

29

THE AIR STIRRED, CARRYING THE FAINT RUBBER SCENT OF TIRES. The front of the bike was a giant Ferris wheel, spinning against the darkness of the zigzag trees. And beside the bike was a tall black column—rounded shoes, and cloth, and a deep sound of breathing.

Emma.

It was a guess. The highest thing Robert could see, when he looked up, was the pale underside of a chin, jutting like overhanging rock. But it had to be Emma. He held his breath, willing her to look down. Willing her to see the petals they had taken so long to lay out.

The huge wheel rolled toward them and stopped suddenly. Still staring up, Robert saw the massive head tilt downward. He heard the noise of rushing air—a sharp, startled breath.

It was Emma, and she was staring down at the pattern on the concrete.

Robert looked, too, seeing it for the first time in the light. The colors sang against the black of the oily concrete.

The great circle they had made was almost too big for him to take in. Its center was a disc of tiny florets—thirty-four clumps of them, merged into a single, rich brown mass. From that center, hundreds of orange petals radiated outward, ring after ring, exploding into brilliance. It was a vast, glowing marigold, enormous and unmistakable.

And next to it, dwarfed by comparison, was a solitary, pink Herb Robert flower.

A giant Emma and a tiny Robert.

Let her see. . . . Let her understand. . . .

Her head was clearly visible now, its mass of carroty hair fallen forward around the face, every strand thick as a cable. It was Emma, and she'd seen the petals. She *had* to understand.

The huge black figure stood motionless for a second before there was any reaction. When the reaction came, it was horribly, appallingly wrong.

A ferocious shout erupted high above Robert's head. The words were too deep, too loud for him to understand, but he recognized the rhythm of them, even with his hands clapped over his ears.

She was furious. She was out of control, yelling over her shoulder at someone he couldn't see. Her dark shape shook terrifyingly, and a torrent of noise flooded back toward the house.

Then one of her great black shoes lashed out, kicking at the ground and scattering the petals, grinding them into the concrete. The heavy, ridged sole crashed down so close that Robert heard Cam shout a warning at him. But he was beyond being careful. He was burning up with frustration and despair.

She hasn't *understood! She hasn't understood a thing! It was all a waste—all that time and planning and energy. Cam was right. They're too different from us. We can't make contact with them. They're too different. . . .*

Red rage swept over him, choking out everything else, and

his hand reached out blindly, feeling for his spear. In that instant, he would have thrown a dagger, a grenade—even a bomb if he'd had one. He would have hit out with anything that might hurt enough to make him visible. Enough to force her into seeing him. *I'm here! I'm just as real as you are! Look at me!*

But instead of his spear, he found Zak's hand. It closed around his, folding the fingers shut and pushing his arm down to his side. Robert struggled furiously, spinning around to yell at Zak, to mouth what he wanted to say if it couldn't be heard.

Why won't she look at us? I hate her—

But the shout froze on his lips. As he met Zak's eyes, full on, the low light caught them aslant. They flashed bright blue, dazzling, and clear, and for an instant, Robert couldn't see anything else. Only that face, rushing toward him out of the black tunnels of his own eyes.

It was you. . . .

The knowledge knocked the breath out of him. Everything that had happened spun in his head. Pain and fear and confusion. Struggle and beauty and death. His brain boiled with questions, too many to speak, too many ever to disentangle.

Zak's lips moved, shaping a single word.

Now.

The sound was blotted out by the roar around them, but Robert heard it inside his head, as clearly as though it had been spoken into silence. And he understood that this was the moment he had come for.

This is the place where I can change things.

Slowly, still in that silence, he turned back and saw another huge figure coming through the gate. Its shoes were like Emma's, massive and black, with toes like steep, rounded hills. But these toes were scuffed bare and there was a long groove scratched into the side of one of them.

He knew that scratch. It was twice as long as his whole body now, but he recognized the ugly, upward line and the shallow, hooked scrawl at the end. He'd done it when the shoe was new, catching his foot against a broken railing.

The second figure stopped beside the first. Robert saw its head move, looking down at the concrete. It turned from side to side, taking in the squashed mess of marigold petals and the little pink flower lying off to one side.

Zak's fingers tightened around Robert's hand for an instant. Then they loosened and withdrew, leaving him free to step forward. Robert was more afraid than he had ever been, through all the strangeness that had gone before. But he wasn't nervous. He knew exactly what he had to do.

He stepped away from the wall and began to walk steadily out across the concrete. The sound above him thinned for a second, and he caught the sound of Cam's voice, shouting high and shrill.

"Robert! You can't—"

But he didn't stop. He went on walking, all the way across the concrete, until he reached the little pink Herb Robert flower. Then he turned. He turned away from Cam and Zak toward the two huge shapes and the great spoked wheels of the bicycles.

He was totally visible, completely exposed and vulnerable. The dusty brown of his skin stood out clearly against the black surface of the oily concrete. If the vast eyes above kept staring down, they couldn't miss seeing where he was. And what he was.

The flowers had made a picture of that, an image of the unknown, to draw attention. But now he was there himself, more real than any image, small and unprotected. They could choose to recognize him and be disturbed. Or they could simply march on, trampling him under their feet.

That wasn't his decision. All he could do was make himself visible. He stretched out his arm and touched the nearest petal of the flower that carried his name.

There was one last rumble above him, deep and sharp, and then complete silence. In the silence, the scratched shoes ahead of him began to flex. They bent into heavy creases across the center as their heels rose off the ground.

The huge, unthinkable figure who wore those shoes began to concertina, like a high-rise building folding itself away. The knees and the head came down and forward, and the great pale face hung over him like an asteroid, its surface rough and irregular. The mouth opened into a cave with quivering walls, big enough to swallow him up a dozen times over. The nostrils gaped like tunnels disappearing into the dark, with hairs clustered inside the entrance.

And the eyes—

Tilting his head back as far as it would go, Robert stared up at them. Their rounded surfaces gleamed wet and vast flicked by eyelashes like rigid wires, thick as his fingers. Their pupils were windows into darkness. The irises were gray-green, striped in a dozen places with faint brown lines. Individual as a fingerprint. They quivered and drew back, contracting as the eyes opened wider.

From the darkness of the pupils, Robert saw a tiny, mud-stained figure staring back at him. For a second he was looking into the dark cavern, and the figure was Lorn in her old bat-leather tunic. *So small, so small* . . . She was pale with hunger, and the bones stood out sharply in her cheeks.

I will do anything to stop that, he thought. *Anything.*

Lifting up his arms, he stretched them toward her. The reflection moved to match, and he understood that he was seeing not Lorn but himself, reaching out and up.

A pale shape separated itself from the great mass above him, moving out and down to meet his hand. As it came through the air, he saw that it was a hand, too. It was grotesquely large—big enough to crush him to a pulp—but it was still a hand, just like the one that he was holding up. He went to meet it, reaching up toward the vast, outstretched fingers.

"Robert! No!"

Cam's shriek reached him, even in the silence. When he looked around, he saw that she was distraught. Zak was holding her around the waist to keep her from running across to him.

"Don't do it! Robert! Don't!"

As she yelled, the great hand above Robert moved down so close that he could feel the heat coming off it and see the ridged patterns of the skin. He reached up, deliberately, and touched it, fingertip to fingertip.

I will do anything. . . .

Immediately the world around him began to contract. Looking back, he saw Cam and Zak shriveling, like snails drawing back into their shells, like balloons collapsing, like buildings dwindling into nothing as an airplane suddenly tilts upward off the ground and climbs into the sky. They were shrinking away from him, disappearing into nothing, vanishing. . . .

A wind roared into him, blowing up through his bones to howl in the empty spaces of his heart.

Cam . . . Zak—
Cam, Zak, Lorn, Dess, BandoTinaAnnetPerdewLornAb
ShangLorn—
Forlorn, perdu desolate abandoned where who lost
Lost
    Lost
        Lost . . .

THE WIND BLEW HIM APART, EXPLODING HIM OUTWARD, straining at every limb and ligament. He was pulled thin and wide, stretched taut enough to reach around the world, from one hemisphere to another.

It was gone, it was gone. Cam and Zak had shrunk away beyond recall, beyond seeing, and it was all over it was finished and gone but he didn't want . . . it was too soon . . . he wasn't ready . . . and he didn't want . . . he didn't want—

AND THEN HE WAS FALLING, CRUMPLING DOWN AND DOWN and down to the ground, and Emma was bending over him and shouting into his face.

"Rob! What's the matter? What's happening? *Rob!*"

And he was falling—

30

In the cavern, Lorn slept late, dreaming in Zak's place by the tunnel mouth.

She stood in darkness, desperately braiding a multi-stranded rope with sluggish, aching fingers. Every twist of the fibers sapped her energy; every turn drained life away from her. But she kept braiding, watching the rope snake away from her, out through the tunnel and down into the ravine.

Hoarfrost was gathering along her knuckles, and icicles were forming under her nails. With every movement, the cold bit deeper, and the pain increased. But she went on lifting and twisting and pulling and lifting and twisting. . . .

She knew, without turning to look, that the others were clustered close behind her in the darkness, feeding the threads into her hands. And at every moment, at every movement, her brain cried out, *I can't . . . they have to understand I can't. . . .* But the words stayed unspoken and the rope fed out through her hands, inch by inch, creeping on and on into the cold.

I can't, I can't. . . .

She woke suddenly, rigid and sweating, with the dim shape of the cavern roof above her, ringed by familiar, anxious faces looking down. Bando and Perdew. Annet and Dess. Ab and Shang and Tina . . .

It was then, in that last second of her sleep—when she came out of the dream with her eyes open but her fingers still moving to the pattern of the braid—that she felt something tug at her hands. Her fingers tightened around the rope, feeling it taut.

As though someone had taken hold of the other end at last.

after

31

When Robert came to, his arm was looped over Emma's shoulders and she was pulling him toward the side gate, half carrying and half dragging him. The shoes were heavy on his feet, and the cloth of his trousers rubbed at the insides of his knees.

Emma was scolding him under her breath. "What's up with you? We're going to be *so late* for school. If you hadn't messed around with the marigolds—Rob, are you all right?"

No, he wanted to say. *No, I have lost everything. I'm different now, and I shall never see them again.* But words were beyond him. His body was weak and shaking, and his mind was sick with the memory of Cam and Zak, shrinking away from him. Sick with the knowledge that if he called to them now, they wouldn't hear anything except a distant, thunderous rumble.

"Rob!" Emma put her head close, whispering in his ear.

And if they spoke, he would not hear their voices either. They were too faint and shrill for his ears to register. He would never hear any of them again.

"Rob, I can't go on taking your weight like this. Try to stand up."

By the time Emma got through to him, they had reached the back door, and she was trying to support him with one hand and find her key with the other. Robert rolled away from her arm and propped himself against the wall.

There was a small, pink flower crushed against the front of

his jacket. He picked it off and looked at it stupidly, struggling to see what he had seen before. When Emma opened the door, he stumbled into the kitchen and slumped down in the nearest chair.

"What on earth is the matter?" Emma said. "Are you ill?"

Robert didn't know what to say. He was aching and exhausted and stunned with shock and grief. Was that *ill*? He looked at Emma blankly across the kitchen table.

"Oh, for goodness' sake!" she said. "Have a cup of coffee and pull yourself together!"

She got up to put the coffeepot on, and Robert laid his head down on the table. Just for a rest. While he was waiting.

When he woke up, he was still in the kitchen, and Emma was sitting on the other side of the table, staring at him.

"About time," she said.

Robert rubbed his eyes and looked at the clock. He had been asleep for two and a half hours. Had Emma been sitting there all the time, waiting for him to wake up?

"Sorry." He rubbed his eyes again. "Did I miss the coffee?"

She made some more, and they sat facing each other. Each one waiting for the other to begin.

"Well?" Emma said at last.

Robert put his mug down on the table. "What did you see?" he said carefully. "When I—when we were outside? Tell me what happened."

Emma looked down. "I came through the gate and saw that someone had vandalized all the marigolds and I thought—well, it just had to be you. With the Herb Robert being there as well. That's why I shouted. And then you went all . . . strange." She lifted her head and met his eyes, edgy and aggressive. "What was going on? Was it supposed to be some kind of *joke*?"

He could hear the fear in her voice. She was offering him a way to cover up, to reassure her that nothing weird had happened after all. All he had to do was bat it back at her. *The trouble with you is, you've got no sense of humor. If you'd seen your face—*

It would be easy to say that. To let her duck out of the extraordinary, inconceivable evidence of her own eyes. *You're such a sucker. . . .* Once the words were out, she would be able to believe that she "knew" what had "really" happened. And by tomorrow he would be starting to believe the same thing himself.

And it would all be over.

If that was what he wanted.

But it was real. . . .

He looked at her, willing her to talk about the strange, unsettling thing she had seen—so that he would know it was all right to tell her the rest. But she didn't give way. She looked back warily, waiting for him to speak.

It has to be now.

Robert took a deep breath. "I wasn't joking," he said evenly. "And I didn't 'vandalize' your flowers. I picked them because I needed to attract your attention. And it took me all night to do it. With two other people to help me."

Emma was very still. Robert picked the small pink flower off his knee, where it had fallen while he was asleep. He laid it on the table, smoothing the petals with one finger.

"Tell me what you really saw," he said.

Emma stared down at the flower. He couldn't believe she was going to tell him. He couldn't imagine her saying anything like that. But he went on waiting, and after a long pause she began to talk. Speaking in a low voice, very quickly, so that he had to concentrate to catch the words.

"I came out and saw the mess on the concrete. I was mad, because I *knew* it was you. So I started to shout—" She broke off short and slid her hand toward the flower on the table. Almost touching it.

"And then?" Robert said.

"Then you came through the gate, with that stupid, blank expression you've had ever since—"

"Since we came back from vacation?"

Emma nodded angrily. "It's been like talking to a brick wall. And seeing you like that then was the last straw. So I just opened my mouth and yelled. And—"

She broke off again. This time Robert didn't prompt her. He just waited and, after a moment or two, she slid her hand another inch and touched the pink flower. She went on talking, without looking up.

"When you saw the flowers—the big marigold and this little one—you just ignored me. Completely. As if you couldn't even hear my voice. You squatted down, quite slowly, and reached your hand out to touch the flower, the way I'm touching it now. And—"

Her voice shook, and Robert thought she was going to faint. He reached out and put his hand on top of hers. "Go on," he said.

"You'll think I'm crazy—"

256

"Go *on!*"

It came all in a rush. As though she had to get the words out while she dared to do it. "There was a little . . . a little *thing* by the flower. When you touched the flower, you touched the thing as well, and it started to grow and it all happened very fast, but— It was *you*. And for a second, just for a second—" She looked up and met his eyes, struggling to finish.

"For a second there were two of us?" Robert said.

Emma nodded. And then shook her head fiercely. "But there can't have been. That's not how things *are*."

"Maybe they can be like that," Robert said carefully. "I hope so. Otherwise I've been raving mad for the last three months."

Emma hesitated for a moment, like someone standing on the brink of a precipice. Then she said, "And if you're not crazy?"

Robert leaned forward, with his elbows on the table, and began to tell her everything, right from the beginning.

When he had finished, Emma sat back in her chair and folded her arms. She looked at him for a long time without speaking. Then she said, "Do you mean it? It's all real?"

"Yes," Robert said. "It's real."

"But how—? Why—?"

Robert shook his head. In his mind, Zak's eyes flashed blue and challenging, and the big unanswered questions screamed down toward him, too big to understand. But he wasn't ready to think about them. Not yet.

"So—what are you going to do?" Emma said.

Lie down and sleep, Robert wanted to say. He knew there were things to do, but he was so tired that he could hardly think. He shrugged again.

Emma looked impatient. "For goodness' sake! You can't just sit around. We've got to do something. To help the others survive."

She jumped up and began to pull things out of the cupboard and the fridge, piling them onto the table. Sugar. Rice. Currants. A package of bacon and a box of cookies. Pasta and a box of matches.

"We can stock them up for the winter!" she said excitedly.

Robert looked down at the heap on the table and thought, *She is too different. She can't understand.*

"Well? *Say* something!" Emma was starting to look frustrated. "What's the problem? We can take them food and blankets—well, maybe not blankets, but you know what I mean—and something to help them heat the cavern and— we've got so *much!* It's easy for us to help."

Robert didn't know where to start. She had it all wrong. There was no room for all those supplies in the small, moist space inside the cavern. The matches and the sugar would get damp. The rice and pasta were useless without a pot to boil them in. The bacon would go bad long before it was finished, and the smell would attract hordes of predators.

She is too different.

Emma was watching his expression. "We've got to do something," she said. "If it really *is* real. We can't just let them die."

Robert looked at Emma's eager, impatient face and thought what an effort it would take to explain everything to

258

her. Then he stared down at the things on the table, trying to figure out how they could be made useful.

Because he did understand—because he was different but not different—he saw what a huge undertaking it would be. How much time and effort and perseverance it would need. The thought of it was like a great weight. *Why me?* But he knew the answer already.

Because he was different but not different, he was the only one who could do it properly.

And he'd promised. *I'll do whatever it takes,* he'd said.

He looked back at Emma's expectant face and began the long, slow process of explaining things that seemed too obvious to need explaining.

"We can't save them with one giant food parcel. That would be easy for us, but it would just make things worse for them. What they need is a little at a time. Food and wood and something to keep them warm." *What would do that? Dry cotton batting, maybe. Constantly replaced.* "We'd have to go every few days or so."

He expected Emma to argue, but she didn't. She hesitated for a second and then nodded. "We could do that. It would take a bit more effort, but we could do it."

"All through the winter?" Robert said. Watching her face. She didn't waver. "I don't see why not."

Robert went on relentlessly. "And what then? Do we give up after one winter? Or do we carry on for two? Or three? What if we want to go away to college?" He saw her eyes change as she took in the size of the commitment, but he didn't stop. "Think about it properly. We can't change our minds when it gets difficult or when we get bored. It's not a game, Emma. It's *real*. It's about people's lives. Ours as well as theirs."

That did get through. For a moment he thought she was going to back out and leave him to do it all on his own.

Then she reached for the packet of currants.

"How many of these shall we take today?" she said.

3 2

THEY WENT OUT AN HOUR BEFORE THE PARK CLOSED, CARRYING one little bag of food and a small piece of dry cotton batting. As they came out of the front garden, Robert stopped for a moment to pick two marigold leaves. He laid them on the ground by the end of the wall, one on top of the other, with a few fragments of bread and cheese hidden between them. Supplies for the journey back.

He hoped that Cam and Zak would find them before the birds did.

Then he and Emma went across the road and into the park. It took them a couple of minutes to walk through the tall trees by the gate. They stepped over the little stream and followed the path by the cypress hedge, along the side of the grass.

At the far end of the park, the hedge changed to a mixture of holly and hawthorn and beech. They found a way through and stepped over the ditch, into the small, brambly wood.

"Where now?" Emma said.

For a moment, Robert's brain struggled to translate *this* into *that*. Then he looked along the ditch and saw a dead, dry stalk of cow parsley, bent over at the base. It would have bridged the ditch, except that it was broken in the middle.

The pain hit him, just as he knew it would. Sharp as the stab of a knife.

Lost—

"There," he said.

There were dozens of little holes all along the hedge bank. When they came to the right place, he sniffed at the air, catching a faint, frail smell of wood smoke (Or did he imagine it?). Then he crouched down and tried to think small, to remember the exact shape of the ground outside the tunnel entrance.

When he was sure, he knelt in front of the hole, and Emma came and knelt down beside him, with the little bag in her hand.

"What now?" she said. "Do we just leave it all on the ground?"

Robert shook his head. "Something else will get it if we do. I want to make sure."

He looked into the hedge for a dead, beech twig. There was a long, straight one off to the right, just above his head, and he reached up and snapped it off, between his finger and thumb. Taking out the food and the cotton batting, he laid them on the ground in front of the hole.

Then, very slowly and carefully, he pushed each thing gently into the hole, using the beech twig he had picked.

When everything was in, he broke the stick into small pieces—as small as he could manage with his big fingers—and stacked them up by the tunnel entrance. Then he stood up.

"That's it," he said. "Until next week."

Emma looked down at the little stack of wood. "We'll never see them. Will we?"

"No," Robert said. "We won't see them. We're too big."

"Do you think they'll ever—I mean—" Emma struggled

with the words. "If you've made it back home, does that mean they might—?"

The flash of hope was so painful that Robert didn't think he could bear it. *Lorn . . .* He closed his eyes and blanked out his mind, thinking of Nate beside the brazier. *What had he said? We don't* remember. *We look forward.*

For the first time, it seemed like a tempting option.

Emma patted his hand and stood up. "Come on," she said. Her voice was gentler than he'd ever heard it. "Let's go back home." She jumped over the ditch and set out toward the break in the hedge.

As Robert followed her, the broken cow parsley stalk caught at the bottom of his jeans. Bending down to flick it off, he realized suddenly that there was one more thing he could do to be useful. Now that he was *big enough*.

He walked along the hedge, looking for another strong, straight stalk. When he found one that was suitable, he broke it off and brought it back to lay across the ditch. Its dry, spreading crown settled firmly onto the earth, and for one, unnerving moment, he saw it with double vision.

Flick. It was a strong bridge, linking two sides of a deep ravine.

Flick. It was a brittle stalk that he could snap between two fingers.

He held both pictures in his mind and the clamoring questions screamed down again, ready to rip the world apart. Slowly he walked his fingers along the stalk, right across to the other side of the ditch, feeling the ridged surface and the little, stiff hairs.

I remember, said the voice in his head. *I remember . . .*

He let himself hear it, not trying to escape the pain. Opening his mind to all the questions.

Then he stood up and went through the gap in the hedge and out onto the grass. Jogging slightly, to catch up with Emma.